Happiness Comes From Nowhere

Shauna Gilligan

Ward Wood Publishing
www.wardwoodpublishing.co.uk

Published by Ward Wood Publishing
6 The Drive
Golders Green
London NW11 9SR
www.wardwoodpublishing.co.uk

The right of Shauna Gilligan to be identified as the author of this work has been asserted by her in accordance with the Copyright, Designs and Patent Act, 1988. © Shauna Gilligan 2012.

ISBN 978-1-908742-03-2

British Library Cataloguing in Publication Data. A CIP record for this book can be obtained from the British Library.

Designed and typeset in Garamond
by Ward Wood Publishing.

Cover Design by Mike Fortune Wood
Cover Photograph: © Xuan Busto www.asturphoto.com

Printed and bound in Great Britain
by Imprint Digital, Seychelles Farm,
Upton Pyne, Exeter EX5 5HY.

For Isolina, Fionn and Xuan

In memory of Seán Gilligan

Happiness Comes From Nowhere

Prologue

The white round tablets with the little line down the middle tumbled in *easy peasy* with a few gulps of whiskey. Holding several in his trembling hand, he visualised them sliding down his throat before skiing through his oesophagus, a bitter edge to them. *Weee* they would go. *Weee.* Like going in a too-fast car over a bump on a winding country road. *Weee.* He laughed; more of a splutter than a proper laugh as they continued to go in.

The psychologist he saw years ago had told him to visualise calm things at times of stress so that it would be easier for him to cope. Think of a beach. Imagine the waves. Remember something from your childhood. Something of comfort. Soothing. The image of his mother's lilac silk flowery blouse blowing on the line on that windy morning came to mind as Dirk Horn listened to the echo of the crunching rebound in his ears, the involuntary shudder, the accompanying jaw-ache somewhere in the distance.

As he'd leaned, half-asleep, against the dirty bus window on the way home from the gig that September evening, his head bouncing off the pane, he had tried to imagine what he would be thinking, how he would feel when he swallowed the painkillers. Would he be filled with fear, tinged with regret, or riddled with guilt? Would he be excited at the prospect of becoming a tragic hero at such a young age? He had watched the scenes of the Dublin suburbs on a Friday night fade away. He was surprised at his complete indifference to the capital; the place that had kept him cocooned and entertained.

He wouldn't miss it at all. Not the darkness of the city or the sounds of the young wandering the back streets with their newly earned degrees; idle, bored and penniless, searching for the next big thing. The way the smell of crisps mixed with the earthiness of Guinness lingered on his fingers, like an exotic tobacco. He wouldn't even miss the guitar riffs roaring from the pubs, the stench of booze and smoke mixed with sweat, Old Spice and Charlie as the crowds called for more. More, more, more. Communal happiness replacing the individual feeling of hopelessness. More, more, more.

Shivering and alone, now seated on the edge of his bed, the hand-knitted bedspread slightly crooked, he shoved in another few, the bitter taste no longer seeming so bitter. The predominant feeling was not one of fear – he had always thought that when death came he would be terrified – or even of regret or excitement, but one of a deep serenity (a serenity that had existed all along, he now thought) which had forced its way up from beneath the weeds of depression that had been strangling him. And mixed with this gentle peace, like the advert for the fabric softener (the name of which now escaped him), was a sensation of smoothness. Yes, he thought to himself, smiling, the pupils of his eyes widening as the realisation struck him; he himself was silk, smooth as silk, the smooth operator he'd always fancied being, the man about town he'd pretended to be.

Physically it was hard work. He needed to get a decent amount of them into his system as quickly as he could. If he stopped now, he knew he wouldn't finish. He shovelled them in, the whiskey splashing everywhere. He thought he was like a starving infant eating warmed apple purée; he couldn't get them in fast enough, half swallowed whole, parts falling back out of his mouth. His body began to heave. He glanced quickly at the plastic white thing from which he poured the tablets – what was it? A box? A bottle? A jar? He suddenly couldn't remember what it was called. What the hell was it called? He could feel himself panicking. He, a librarian, surrounded by words, by letters, could not remember the name of a simple everyday item.

His heart beat faster and he rubbed the back of his neck, his hand mopping the sweat that was drenching him. He breathed out slowly, trying to quell the panic and regret. No. But then, he smiled to himself as he burped up the taste of Budweiser, that all-American-feel-good beer (God, he thought, it was great tonight) mixed in with whiskey: semantics, what did it matter? And he was pleased – half way but another half of the stuff in the plastic thing to go. At the end of the day, he could always paint it. Paper, canvas, whatever – it could still *exist*.

Nearly there, he thought, as the helicopters in his head whirred louder. He looked down at his feet, glad to see they were naked; he must have kicked his dirty runners off. And his beige socks. Good, that was something; if nothing else, he had done right for his mother. Always remove your footwear before getting into or onto a bed. The ends of his jeans – he always had trouble finding ones with a short enough leg – were worn from him standing on them; he really had to do something about it. He could feel himself getting anxious again; it wouldn't do to leave looking shabby or unkempt and forgetting the name of the thing that contained the tablets that would kill him.

He picked up the torn playlist he had scrawled on earlier that evening, shouting that he had the perfect solution, like a dictator ignoring the real problem, which was himself. He was a criminal, he realised. This was Ireland in the early '90s. He could be prosecuted for taking his own life. He spluttered; you couldn't prosecute the dead. All he was doing was searching for happiness. What was so wrong with that?

Suicide at any age is an unspeakable tragedy but at such a young age is almost unthinkable. 'Why', the question that burned on this man's lips before the deed was done. 'Why' or was it 'why not'? ~~It might be said about the case of Dirk Horn, stolen from us in his prime, that this suicide is, in fact, a brave and noble act.~~ It causes much pain and leaves unanswered questions for those left behind: Angela – Mary – etc etc. ~~The reality for us all is that~~ Mother, Mammy, Mary. There is nothing left to say. I'm sorry, sorry for all of it.

He looked at his scrawl, smiled at the unfinished sentence echoing his life. *The reality for us all is that* – What was he thinking when he stopped writing that line? It wasn't anyone's reality, only his own. He was the one who spoiled the parties, who couldn't bring himself to love the girl he had convinced himself was the perfect one for him. He was the one. He was the one in his bedroom drinking. Alone. He remembered a photograph he'd looked at often; it was on a wall in the house and always made him smile. He was about four, on his mother's shoulders, at a St Patrick's Day parade. He remembered his father's smiling face when he took the photograph. Then he'd nearly fallen backwards into the crowd. His parents had laughed and he'd hugged them both. A small arm around each neck. He felt the happiness of that moment, then, as if it were only yesterday. And a shudder of grief passed through his body.

In the back of his mind somebody was retching and moaning and he was asking himself what exactly was brave about swallowing a bunch of paracetamol after having taken your runners off and that really he should remove Angela (he'd even forgotten to give her the respectability of capitalising her name) when suddenly the whirring became deafeningly loud. Waves of nausea came, pushing him away, pushing harder and harder, stronger and stronger, his head filled with the pains of a million hangovers. Any sense of fear or panic were forced away by the approaching blackness and the overriding thunder of his heartbeat.

It was like floating on the sea, feeling the sparkle of the sun as it bounced off his body, his eyes closed. He was nothing if not at peace. There was a silence like he had never heard before. It was like when his ears used to pop as a child when he was up high in the mountains and the world suddenly seemed a more bearable place. It was a beauty. This silence was what they called eternal peace.

Yet, there was something fundamentally wrong about the situation that he now found himself in. And the thoughts that he thought he was thinking were not thoughts, really, because he was not there, but driftings, whisperings, like angels or fairies hovering above him, shaking their heads in dismay; those beings we insist on denying, as they looked down upon yet another misled and misunderstood youth unable to ask for help; never heard when the cry (of reawakening) finally erupted from his mouth.

Then there was silence.

And darkness.

Later, a loud thud could be heard in an upstairs bedroom of a period house in south county Dublin on the third of September. The local librarian, Dirk Horn, his face veiled in sweat and covered in his own vomit, his stomach full of painkillers, beer and whiskey, its instinct to empty itself kicking in, regret slipping into his consciousness, slid off his childhood bed onto the moss-coloured carpet, having proclaimed a ceasefire with his demons.

The Only Baby

Mamá. Mother. Mam. Mammy. Mháthair. Mutter. Mutti.

Words. Words perfectly formed but sounding like a culture I knew nothing about; a language I could speak but not understand. None of the words for mother sat easy with me. I took to reciting them with the idea that, in time, hearing *Mother* would come as natural to me as responding to the *come here* of my husband Sepp when he was in the mood.

The nightly recitals of the phonetics of motherhood did not sit easy between us. But his arms still circled me as mine wrapped around the bump. 'You know,' he told me, 'it's the hormones, not you.' He reached down and replaced my hand with his. I could feel the baby moving with the change of temperature; his hand was freezing. 'This baby is a strong one, I can tell.' I pulled away. How could he tell our child was strong? It was growing in *my body*. I was the mother; I should know what the child would be like, not him. As much as I searched, the only feeling that I had about this baby was that it was a boy. I knew it was a boy. With no emotion attached to this knowledge, no sense of what type of boy or what joy or sorrow he might bring us. But Sepp knew. Sepp knew he would be strong, strong and different. Sepp, whose eyes narrowed in suspicion when he looked at the bump, whose eyes lit up when his hand stroked my skin that had grown with the baby inch by inch. It was my skin, my body which housed this being; my mind which processed the changes with vivid cinematic dreams.

'I can feel the baby kicking,' Sepp would say, his voice credulous, as if I couldn't feel it too, as if he'd discovered something for the first time. 'I can feel it!'

'You shouldn't do that,' I said to him one day. 'It's bad for the baby. Only the mother should touch the bump.' I looked at my body, which had ballooned out far more than any of the pregnant women in the books I was reading. The doctor had smiled sweetly and said that each and every woman's body reacts differently to pregnancy; some women are *bigger* than others.

Sepp stood, frowning, hands on hips, his silver-grey work suit with complementary lilac shirt looking foolish at home. 'What?'

'The doctor said,' I lied, my voice chirpy, 'he said it's bad.' I took a breath. 'He also said it's good to get exercise. I'm off to Bushy Park with Sheila so you might like to leaf through this.' I flung *The Continuum Concept* at him.

'And you might as well be married to that sister of yours the amount of time you spend with her,' he snapped each word out in his lovable German staccato.

*

'You don't have to give up smoking. I mean they don't know if it harms the baby. Give yourself a break – I mean, you can't completely change your life even before it's born!'

'But I want to, Sheila. I've entered into a new state of being.'

'A new state of being? Ah, now come on.'

I shrugged. The ducks were making their way across the lake towards us, oblivious to our indifference as we started along the circular path which ran alongside it.

'You know, that's what it feels like. It's the biggest change I've ever gone through.'

'What, bigger than running away to Germany? Bigger than missing Mammy's funeral just because you fell in love? You've done some big ones in your life, Mary. Pregnancy is an easy one.'

Sheila scuffed the ground with her perfectly white runner.

'Yeah and you'd know, wouldn't you?' I grimaced; I'd offended her. She'd always wanted children and with no man on the horizon it was looking like she'd never have any. I laughed lightly. 'I mean, you'd think, wouldn't you, given the fuck-ups so far – but this is a biggie. The difference is that I'm not in control.'

She looked at me, peering at the bump. Her summer freckles

had faded a little; my little sister had developed a few more wrinkles, but those blue eyes still had that sparkle of mischief in them. She had her strawberry blonde hair tied back with a scrunchie in a sharp ponytail; too sharp for her age, I thought. At just gone thirty, she still wore her hair the same way as Mother had made her wear it aged three. At just gone thirty, she still slept in the same bedroom we had shared as girls. We were peas in a pod, the McNamara girls with eighteen months between us, but different peas the way we lived our lives. But still, we got on, especially since I'd come back from Germany married to the man I'd run away for; the good-looking tall, dark and handsome stranger who spoke perfectly correct English.

Sheila reached out to touch the bump and drew back her hand. Her cheeks reddened. 'You're massive.'

'All baby, baby, baby.'

She looked away and muttered. 'You must wish Mother were here.'

A dog chased ducks. Sheila called it back. A Labrador – it turned to look at her and then raced off again. 'That dog should be on a leash.' She frowned.

I smiled. 'What harm?'

Two overly-thin women in lemon yellow towelling tracksuits jogged past us. Sheila rolled her eyes, walked faster.

'Sure, what would I ask her if she were here?'

'Her pregnancies. They say your body responds to the hormones like your mother's did.'

'And if she were here she'd be all over me like a rash. *Don't do this, don't do that, you're growing a baby.*'

Sheila smiled. 'She's got to be looking after this one.'

'Hang on.' I stopped walking, trying to catch my breath. 'Jesus, I need a bench.'

'Come on, we've nearly done the round. You can sit at the end.'

'There's exercise and there's – '

'Come on!'

I smiled. 'So she had us two and then she lost three, well three that we know of. I mean, how can I tell which one of the five pregnancies this one will be like?'

Sheila shrugged.

'She's probably rolling her eyes wondering why it's me and not you.'

'Now you've said it. Here I am permanent and pensionable in the Civil Service and you who hated kids – '

'I never hated them – '

' – but you never wanted... '

'It wasn't that I never wanted them... I just... never thought about them.'

'Bullshit. You wanted to be an astronaut or a scientist.'

'Yeah, and then did literature.'

'Who was to say you couldn't read in space or be a scientist who read books?'

'And look at me now. The house filled with books on babies.'

Sheila clapped her hands. 'House filled with books. What did I say?'

I put my arm around her shoulders. 'Thanks.'

She pushed me off. 'What do they say then, all these books?'

'That I should expect change. That I have to get the baby into a routine. I should never hold the baby because that will teach it bad habits. I should breastfeed and keep the baby in my arms all the time where it will feel safe.'

'Jesus. How do you know which is the right way?'

'I've no clue.'

'Well then you should just follow your instinct.'

'Yeah, that great instinct of mine for fuck ups.'

'This one isn't a fuck up. Here.' She handed me a menthol cigarette.

I hesitated and she laughed. It was probably the best cigarette I had ever smoked. We laughed as we linked arms and finished our lap around the lake.

'Right,' I said as the park gates came into view, 'forget the bench. We're going to the chipper, like it or not.'

I'd developed a real *grá* for chipper chips, smothered in vinegar and covered in salt – better than that, I couldn't get. We got our chips and walked home, like teenagers again, burning our fingers and tongues, the grease sticking to our teeth, the salt

15

like an exotic lipstick.

*

The baby was in tune with me; he was copying my routines. It was a slow dawning, like a performance of Keats' negative capability. It developed of its own accord. Bearing the baby as it grew was like wading through knee-deep snow, trying to run in the sea. I became part of his surrounds. This baby and I were one. We were waddling through time from conception to birth with nothing more important than just *being* and, of course, growing. In our movements we formed the ultimate union. There were times it felt like hundreds of little feet kicking, little boxers pummelling away inside me. When I walked I felt like the baby was pushing his way out, the bouncing pressure he put on me with each step. When I lay down to rest he stopped kicking, otherwise it was a demanding vociferous kicking that would be heard. I sang to him *'ha boo baba ha boo-een'* petting my bump. When I danced with Sepp – we took to waltzing around the sitting room to Frank Sinatra – he twirled in my womb, pointed his perfectly formed toes, enjoying what was within and what was without. He would never have that again, I thought.

I even took up knitting for the first time since Sister Martha in school had made us knit scarves that were far too long for any human to wear. I numbed my bottom on the bus into town where I'd go to a knitting shop in Caple Street. For each new piece I'd stay in the shop casting on, knitting, casting off. A practice run before the real job at home. It took the best part of the day. The girl said she'd never been so busy; me being in the shop surrounded by knitting patterns and mountains of wool attracted more customers. I left with a brand new knitting basket, several patterns for matinee coats, bed coats (for me and Sheila), teddy bears and bedspreads. Over the next few weeks I tapped my way through the clicking needles and created a bedspread for the child. A souvenir of a time when time itself was nothingness, a time when there was no such thing as need.

Sheila just couldn't believe me. 'I never thought I'd see the day. You and knitting needles.' She looked so like Mammy when she smiled it almost brought out the rebel in me. 'You know it'll go in the bin the minute he reaches the teenage years.' She had the tone to boot.

'You must be joking. I'll tell him how my fingers bled knitting it for him. I'll tell him how he squirmed in my belly when I sewed each square together. Then he'll be afraid to throw it away.'

'You could tell him that knitting it was a sacrifice.' She smirked, evidence of Mammy gone. 'Or a bet.'

'That I lost.'

We laughed so much we cried.

And we laughed then at my swollen feet, the ache of my lower back.

*

At night the dread crept up on me like a silent spider, resting there right on my nose, watching my eyelids move as I dreamt that I was being chased by a shadow, unable to run, unable to move, until I woke up screaming, sweating, and brushed the dreams away with a strike of my hand across my nose. The spider, long gone, having sensed a waking on its way. The dream disguised the fear I felt. The secret fear that I really wouldn't be able to cope with this being who would want everything from me, who would want to be with me all the time, who would worship me and for whom I could do no wrong (and that was the real crux, that I could be loved unconditionally by another human being). I felt angry with him (although when the anger welled up *he* became a thing), taking over me like a parasite, rendering me weak, voiceless, without control. I'd read all the textbooks: Dr Spock's revised *Baby and Child Care* and Jean Liedloff's *The Continuum Concept* – the different ends of the spectrum, both of which I would ignore when he arrived – were the coffee table ones I leafed through on a daily basis.

I began to dread not only the labour and birth but also the actual arrival of the baby. What if I genuinely disliked the baby that I had been carrying for so long, and could not bring myself

17

to love it? What if I could not bear to look at its red face all twisted and sweating as it screamed for food, for attention, for nobody but me? What if my initial instinct that I was not cut out for motherhood proved to be true? That the wrong sister had been made into a mother? What if I had made a horrible mistake? What if neither Sepp nor I were fit to be parents? I woke night after night sweating and screaming – I swore there were nests of spiders in the house, crawling, crawling, and their leader sent to walk with its spindly legs all over me. *Get it off me. Off me. Get it out of me, get it out of me.*

I sobbed into Sepp's arms. He held me in silence and I realised that, for the first time in I couldn't tell how long, the baby wasn't kicking my insides into oblivion. I looked up from the wool jumper.

'I can't feel any kicking.'

'That's okay, the baby is probably asleep.'

'No. He kicks all the time.'

'Or she.' Sepp smiled.

'Don't jolly me along.'

'You've probably frightened him with all the emotions. He's tired.'

As he spoke I saw something between disbelief and boredom in his eyes. I felt like slapping him. Him, in his unchanged state, happily rolling over onto his stomach in bed then jogging, showering and off to his fancy office. Him, who was (I was sure) flirting with perfectly groomed secretaries beside the new photocopiers. Him, who thought he knew my body more than I did; the man I once gave up a life for.

'You can't make me change the way I feel,' I shouted at him. 'And you know what? No matter how many times I have to bring this baby into the bed, I won't be the one complaining.'

Sepp shook his head, rubbing his temples.

'You know why? Do you?' I said.

'No.'

'Because before long, he'll be jumping into bed with some other woman and no longer be my baby. That's how it's going to work. I'm going to love this baby like I have loved nobody else.' I was out of breath.

18

'Listen to yourself. You're talking about you and this baby. We will be family of three. Nobody expects things to be perfect. Nobody is trying to dissuade you from anything.'

I shook my head.

He sighed. 'Okay then, I'm going for a walk. For some… space. We both probably need some.'

I hated his calm logic. I watched him practically tear his overcoat from the hook on the wooden coat stand we'd had shipped from an antique shop in Berlin. It wobbled but didn't topple over. He cursed.

I didn't move a muscle until I heard the slam of the front door. And then I sat on the floor and wept.

*

My waters broke as I was washing the dishes after lunch. It was more dramatic than I could have anticipated. The pop the books had explained really was a *pop* like a balloon bursting. And then a slithery feeling as a trickle was followed within the same second by a gush of strangely warm water. It gushed down my legs onto the green and yellow sun and moon lino on the kitchen floor. It was a Monday, Valentine's Day. I tore my yellow Marigold rubber gloves as I clamoured to take them off, the adrenalin rushing through me. My heart pounded with excitement, this was it, this was really it; I would finally see this being. There was not even a hint of dread or fear.

I decided to run a bubble bath to keep myself warm. I can still feel the coldness of the silver buttons on the denim dungarees with the flowers I embroidered on the back pockets as they brushed off my shoulder when I took them off. I climbed slowly into the bath and lay there, the bump floating. I thought about how I would keep the baby safe from the very moment he would worm his way out of my body in the biggest maternity hospital in Dublin. I swished the water around with my feet, the sickly sweet smell making me heady with its strong scent. It was a collectors' item, they said, in the shape of an ice-cream cone; Avon's *Miss Lollypop*. I was mildly surprised that the contractions were bearable even though they seemed very frequent.

By the time Sepp arrived home to the sound of broken pieces of the *Mockingbird* lullaby being screeched upstairs, I'd used nearly a bottle topping up the bath. I listened to his steps, as he called out my name. When he reached the top of the stairs, I heard the familiar curses. I laughed loudly and he fell through the door, his face a mess of concern.

'Jesus,' he said. 'We're going to the hospital now.'

I nodded obediently.

He puffed as he pulled me out. 'Please don't forget – Dietrich Alphonsus for a boy, Flora Maria for a girl.'

I heard the tremor in his voice and I remember watching him like he was a stranger, thinking how handsome he was, so elegant in a tweed suit and coiffed hair, as he helped me out of the bath. He talked incessantly on the way to the hospital. He talked about everything, reminiscing on when we first met in Bamberg where we both worked, fresh out of university. Everything we'd done – from backpacking around the Greek Islands, staying for weeks on Lesvos, to taking corporate jobs – all brought us to this one moment.

'Procreation,' he said, laughing, 'the only aim of life.'

I looked out the window at the shadows of cars, the twilight headlights flitting by like beings in the air. I couldn't register what he'd said, and even when he sighed loudly I traced a smile in the steam on the windowpane, laughing in a whisper of fear at what was to come.

I was whisked off to the delivery suite. I heard Sepp calling to me that he loved me, as they shoved my feet into stirrups and jammed a gas mask over my nose and mouth. *Jesus you would hardly do that to a bloody horse* I thought. I struggled but there really was no point. The midwives would do what they wanted to do. The gas began to kick in. I could hear a moan in the distance as the contractions came in waves, stronger and stronger, one after the other. I could have sworn the flash of headlights went past me. I could have sworn I heard a siren. I was sure I heard screams. I fell asleep. And then I felt pressure. A pressure which took over, turning me into nothing but a body following orders on how to work properly.

'Push. Breathe – ' I heard one of the midwives' voices in my ear. She tore the mask off me.

'One. Two. Three.'

I became nothing but that push, that pressure.

And then there was a silence.

My ears were ringing. I was panting, exhausted.

'A girl,' I heard the doctor whisper.

I felt my throat constricting as I tried to moan. They were wrong. I *knew* I had a boy inside me. I tried to sit up but they had my legs still hanging like pieces of meat. I tried to scream but within seconds they'd pushed the gas mask down on top of me; the smell of it, the feel of the plastic making me gag. And they were scurrying at the end of the bed shouting at each other. I felt the blood rush to my head. I tried to call out to them, to find Sepp. This was wrong. There was a mistake.

And then, above the headiness of everything, I felt something slither between my legs and heard a cry.

'Mrs Horn,' said a midwife taking the mask away. 'Mrs Horn. Congratulations. You have a baby boy.'

'The girl?' I called out to her back as she walked away.

She hung her head.

'The girl?' I shouted. 'The baby was a girl?'

'Now, Mrs Horn – ' the doctor was at my side with a needle; silver it was. 'You've had a traumatic birth, you need to relax, gather your strength for your beautiful healthy baby boy.'

My boy, the one that I had been waiting on, barged into this world at three minutes past midnight, Tuesday 15th February 1970.

After tests and proddings, weighings and checkings, they handed me the baby. A mass of jet-black hair, huge wondrous eyes that would become the bluest of blue, long grasping fingers and what seemed to be the loudest cries in the world.

Sepp was finally led into the room, told he was the father of a little boy. As I watched him walk towards the bed, I felt that I wasn't there. Or rather, I was in the room but far away. I was on the bed but not as me. The woman he saw propped up in bed smiling at him was a stranger with a secret, someone who had been taken over by the pink baby that lay in her arms.

21

There was a roll of cling film wrapped around us, wrapping us up together to keep the bond fresh and lasting. He looked at the two of us and smiled. A rush of contentment surged through my veins; I was untouchable, unreachable except through this baby.

'Well done, my love.' His face was flushed. I noticed specks of dandruff on his dark purple shirt collar. He looked awkward and coy, like he did when he first asked me out. 'You've given us our Dirk and his name is so right for him, isn't it, Mary?'

I was dizzy and the tears poured down my face. The words *Flora Maria*, ran through my head like wild horses.

'I'm a father,' he said, smiling. '*Ich bin ein Vati.*'

The baby cried loudly and he promptly nursed, his crying subsiding, and fell asleep, all seven pounds three ounces of him. I turned to Sepp and told him I loved him, too. The nurse came over and cupped her hand under his elbow.

'It's been a difficult birth,' she said gently. 'Mrs Horn needs rest. Come now,' she coaxed, 'the Doctor wants to have a quiet word with you before you go home.'

He reached out for my hand, touching me lightly. I shivered a little as I watched him walk out the door.

I quietly sang the same broken, invented lullaby I had sung to the baby in my womb. Dietrich Seamus Alphonsus Horn, our *Dirk*. Ruler of the people. Power of the tribe. The strong one.

The baby who was born alive. The only baby I'd let into my heart.

The Illusion of Freedom

What you desperately want, in tandem with time – that illusion of freedom – is for your child to be the best. And get the best. This is the continuum of the maternal embrace: the provision of wholeness, the want of nothing. In exchange for silent mornings, you hand over your four-year-old child to the state to be *educated*. Before this moment, you wallowed. Your son, with flawless soft skin, as a two-and-three-year-old, snuggled deeper into the crook of your elbow, the dip in your collarbone. He nuzzled into your warmth as you talked to him in your perfected 'mother' voice.

You've a sense of treacle dripping, lush and heavy. You become conscious of the desire within this wallowing. And yet you fear (though it ebbs and wanes) the day when he will say goodbye. So you encourage your mini-man to watch his father from the corner of one exposed eye in the knowledge that *he* and not his father is the preferred male in the household. Your husband, a stranger now, rolls his eyes and sighs loudly. It seems he is in a permanent state of irritation as much as you are in one of sweetness. You brush an old image from your mind: laughing with him as you waltzed along the river Regnitz and ahead, ready to greet you, Bamberg's Old Town Hall.

'Don't spoil him like that. He'll turn into a mama's boy.' His voice is gruff without a trace of how it once whispered.

'Like you?' you reply, not able to look at him, pursing your lips as you apply pressure on each stroke of the boy's hair.

You believe his startling eyes are a sign of his impending greatness. Sepp believes in genetics; simply they are from his side of the family. There is no mystery in the boy, he says.

Sheila dotes on him when he giggles. He transports you both to childhood. Two sisters, girls again, fantasising. Things have possibility. Excitement is in the air.

'Isn't he a howl?' she says, her head thrown back, laughing.

'He's such a charmer; they'll be vying for him when he's older.'

'What do you think he'll be?' you ask, suddenly not caring that she's put her claim on him. 'An actor? A politician?'

'A star on the stage,' she giggles. Like his, you think, realising he's inherited, somehow, your sister's childish giggle. 'Oh,' she continues, her face flushed, 'he'll make us our millions and bring us to Hollywood. We'll wear satin to the Oscars; I'll wear red and you'll wear emerald green.'

Your son claps his hands; his eyes bright. And then his fingers, knuckles hidden by smudges of fat, cover his eyes. *Ahhh* he says as he peeps out at you. Sepp shakes his head, muttering disapproval before disappearing into his study. He turns up Beethoven, conducting the maestro from the comfort of his black leather recliner. He's found a way to get back to Germany, you think. Rain patters the windows. You, your sister and your son giggle conspiratorially together about nothing at all. It is a Saturday, like any other Saturday.

*

Laid out in a neatly penned list, your life is perfectly arranged. There's an oil crisis, people marching the streets and you hear on the radio of women your age gathering together, eyes painted shocking blues with long lashes. They travel up North on trains from the Republic and bring back illegal contraceptives. All the talk is of the *pill* as they claim the right to their bodies, fists held high.

Still, you remain here, silent, with the boy holding the household together like the rough tacking you do on the skirts you make. Sepp works in Dublin for a pharmaceutical company. You treat yourself to a gin and tonic every other day. It's a sunny, south-facing house where you are. On a narrow road, which leads, taking a left, into Dublin city centre; or right, to the Dublin Mountains. To the boy it's the only home he's known. There are times when you smile at each other, glad that you have your own memories of different homes where the boy had no part. Other times you forget about the selves you had before his arrival. You've overseen the rewiring of the original

24

1930s mess, tamed the wild garden. Sepp's clearly made his mark on the house: he painted the doorframes cherry red, the garage door canary yellow. And as you prowl the house, pulling the *Superser* heater behind you for warmth, it comes to you: your duty is to nurture him, put a stamp of personality on him. It's a right transferred by the blood of your womb in a code deciphered by mother and son. Everything written from the moment of conception: his due date, his birth date, his love life, his career, his death.

*

The day has come.

The right to education is written in the Constitution and as a citizen, you must cherish all children of the nation. You fear that, when he leaves you, he will not be cherished. At the school entrance there is chaos. Alongside the bicycles and cars, clatters of mothers dressed like you manoeuvre hoards of boys, copies of each other in mud-brown uniforms. As you glance around at the other children, so small, so lost, so *childish,* you suddenly feel it in your bones that he's grand. You follow the arrows towards his classroom.

The boy kisses you lightly on the cheek; the wet, lingering, puppy-like kisses have vanished with time. You hold his hand as he tries to pull away. With the other hand he's waving goodbye. With a smile on his face, he merges with the rows of small grey chairs. On the wall there is a poster with a blue sky and a black bird. *Éan* it says. Bird. You take a deep breath; it would not do to cry.

*

Alone.

You look around the kitchen. The floor with its lemon and lime lino shining. Even though it didn't need it, you've given it a good scrubbing. The press doors are free of finger smudges. You boil the kettle; listen to the hum of the fridge. You put on the radio, listen to Gay Byrne. You even tap your foot in time

25

to a tune he plays. Frankie's one of your favourites. You must root out an old LP, you think. Put it on, have a dance for yourself. You can do that now. You have the time.

You stare at the kitchen door to the hallway. You have the time, you whisper. You slip off your tan t-bar wedges, tip-toe in your stocking feet into Sepp's study. You slide open the drawer full of LPs, running your fingers over and through them as if flicking pages of a book. You lift one out; its edges centring each palm as you carefully rotate it. You run your nail along its grooves. A jagged edge leaves a fine scratch across the black rings. It is beautiful, this imperfection on the sheen of the black. And you slip it back into its sleeve, close the drawer silently. You tap the drawer, waiting. For nothing.

You breathe in. And then you twirl, holding your arms out like you did when you were a girl. You listen carefully to the sound your stockings make against the wool of the carpet as the ball of your foot rotates. You throw your head back and twirl again.

Laughing, you walk slowly to the kitchen, slide your feet into the shoes. You glance at the clock. You have time to make lunch. Surely, the boy will be hungry after his first day at school. Brown bread. And jam, for a treat. You cover them in cling film, smoothing the wrinkles out with your palm. You think maybe later you could make a brack together, a trial run for Halloween. You could wrap coins in greaseproof paper, count them out. You could make flapjacks, let him lick the spoon.

*

'It's like waiting for a hero,' says one mother as you all crowd around the double doors, vying to spot their big boy or girl first.

'Except, instead of the Rolling Stones' autographs, we're hoping for our children's survival in there.' You try to be witty.

She nods but she doesn't smile. For the foreseeable future, these are the people you'll spend time with twice a day. You hope you'll find some common ground, other than the children. Eventually, you suppose, you'll share laughter over scalding tea.

'Here they are,' the woman says without looking at you.

Elbows out, he's winding past the other children in the line. In unconscious imitation, you push your way through the crowd so that you're at the front of the group. You can hear the teacher shouting at him to get into line *right now*. You rush forward, lifting him high off the ground and tucking him into the side of your neck like you would an expensive scarf. He is silent and averts his eyes.

'What's the matter?' you ask as you put him back down on the ground.

You cup his chin in your hand, turning his face to yours. Instead he breaks away, flings himself onto the peacock-blue velour skirt you made for this, his first day at school. Flustered, you move back from the crowd, away from the glances, the boy's sobs getting louder as you stroke his hair. You hold his hand tightly and push against the tide of mothers and children now making their way out of the school.

A teacher stops you. 'The exit is that way.' She smiles sympathetically.

'I'm looking for the headmaster,' you say in your best professional voice.

Her smile disappears.

'Miss Murphy's class,' you quickly add.

She bends down to his level. 'Who's such a big boy in school then?' Her voice is warm, tone soft.

You resist the urge to slap her youthful cheeks. You feel your grip tightening on your *best* boy.

'I'll see if I can find Miss Murphy,' she says.

'I don't think you heard me correctly, Miss. I want to speak to the headmaster, not the teacher who has clearly upset my son.'

From the corner of your eye you see he's no longer crying. He's curling his hair with his index finger the way he does when he's tired or when he wants to listen to you telling tales of the *Fianna* so that he'll dream of eating the salmon of knowledge.

Miss Murphy approaches and is even prettier than this young teacher with whom she exchanges a silent knowing smile. She asks if you're okay; she saw you upset earlier.

You cross your arms across your chest, releasing the boy's hand. 'It's not me who is traumatised on the first day at school! Just take a look at him!'

Your voice is higher-pitched than normal. This is nonsense, the whole scene. You're making what your grandmother called *a holy show* of yourself. Genetics, you think. It *is* to do with genetics. You grab his hand, gripping it tightly again and clear your throat loudly. He looks at his shoes; you know he's imagining they're hooves. You know this, you think, and this woman does not. He stomps his foot. You squeeze him too tightly and he tries to pull away.

'Neigh!' he says, moving his head around.

'Just stay still,' you hiss, releasing him.

'Neigh! Neigh!' he says, again, louder, looking at you, his eyes full of love.

Miss Murphy watches him as he hops from foot to foot. 'It wasn't so bad today, was it?'

'I'm the best boy, Miss Murphy!'

'Won't you come here again?'

He nods, grinning. 'I'm a big boy at school.'

'Well then, as I was saying,' you begin. You pause, embarrassed. 'Sorry to have taken up so much your time. Thank you.'

'You're welcome. And we'll see *you*, big boy, tomorrow.'

She ruffles his hair; he laughs. She nods at you and turns. The sound of her heels clicking like the snap of Frankie's fingers.

'Bye, bye,' he trills after her as he stomps his feet again. 'I've got happy horsey feet! I'm the best horse in the world. Neigh!'

He continues his horsey games as you walk home with him, too aware of the blister forming on your heel. He bounds forward, a dot in the distance, then springs back leaping in the air.

His leather satchel sits on your shoulder.

You count to ten to stop yourself slapping him.

Sparkle

Suddenly I remembered the afternoon I saw our old yellow car, a Mazda, overtake us on a road. I knelt on the back seat, shouting at the window, trying to sing *Breakfast in America*. The man in it had square glasses and sounds of Supertramp oozed out of the windows. He was singing or maybe shouting along to it. I wanted desperately to be in the car with that man instead of having to listen to the boring conversations of my parents. I wanted to shout out the words at the top of my voice like the man.

I wanted to shout.

Vati was gone. Then Mammy faded like a dot.

The nurse guided me down the corridor. The floor was black with sparkles on it. We went down a slope and then I started crying.

'Oh now,' she said.

Oh now *what?* I wanted to know. All that I wanted, then, was to leave and not have to wave at my parents through a glass shutter. Not to have to see *Vati* run out because he didn't want me to see him upset (but of course I knew he was and was trying to hide it). And then her, Mammy, staying for another minute.

Waving but not smiling.

I was about eight. Having my tonsils out. Lots of girls and boys were having theirs out or maybe it was their adenoids, or they were getting grommets in their ears, but we were all there for our operations, and we all waved goodbye through the hatch and the sister said *Oh now* to all of us, and she expected us to nod and smile and be happy that strange men with frowns on their faces were going to cut us open and try to make us work properly again.

Sometimes I think, maybe we're not meant to work properly. Like clocks that go funny. That's just the way they are. Or cats with bits of their tail missing. It's weird but it's just them. And they eat and they sleep and they purr and they're still nice cats. They're still somebody's pet. They belong.

She'd given me a bag. It was camel brown, she said, not beige. I heard someone saying *beige was in* and I thought it sounded like a nice colour. I wanted the bag to be *in* because it sounded good; I didn't want it to be the same colour as an animal. I explained all this to the sister who just frowned at me.

'It's a brown bag,' she said. 'It has what you need: your pyjamas and your toothbrush and your facecloth and *oh*. A book.'

'Books are great,' I said, smiling. 'I'm going to be bored after my operation, aren't I, so I can read my book.'

'You're going to feel sick, Dirk,' she said, 'sick and tired. You're not in hospital because you're well. You're a sick boy and before you get better you'll have to get sicker.'

The minute she said that I thought I was going to get sick all over the sparkles, there and then.

'Don't you go vomiting over the floors,' she said, wagging her finger at me. 'They've just been mopped.'

When I lay in my bed the sheets were tucked too tightly. The toes on my right foot went tingly because they couldn't stretch out. And if I put my arms inside the covers they got stuck. I wondered if this was what it was like being dead in a coffin in the ground in a graveyard.

The boy in the bed beside mine was whimpering. The sounds he was making were like a kitten's and they would have been cute if they hadn't been so sad. Someone, I thought, someone must have broken his heart.

My bed was the end of the row and next to the whimpering kitten-boy was a girl who was the tallest of us all. Her two front teeth were gone and she spoke funny. The boy on the other side of her kept asking her to say *snakes* and then he'd laugh really loud. This was his last night in the hospital so he was excited. The same morning as he was going home, I was going to have my operation.

I wasn't allowed to eat anything or even to have a drink of water. I lay there, listening to my tummy rumble and I tried to think of how I could have a drop of water. Maybe the doctors wouldn't mind a drop. Was this what the African babies we'd given our pennies to in the Trocaire boxes last Lent felt like when they had no water? The kitten-boy was asleep; his whimpering had stopped. I wiggled around until I'd lifted my legs out of the bed. They lay there like they didn't belong to me.

'New boy,' the boy who got the girl to say *snakes* whispered.

'What?'

'Come on.'

And I was out, not a second to lose, my feet touching the cold ground, the sparkles feeling like they were crunchy or hard or strange on the soles of my feet. We put our hands over our mouths and we tiptoed like they did in the *Famous Five*.

We were out of the ward and into the corridor. Our breathing sounded like monsters getting ready to attack. At the end of the long corridor, there was a statue. It looked bright. The gold on the stars was sparkling. A statue of a child was beside it. There was a glow, like a light of fog, around its red clock and on its head it had a funny looking black hat with bobbles all over it.

'Why are you petting that statue?' He was looking at me like there was something wrong with me.

'I like it.' I wanted to take it. Take it and bring it to bed with me. Maybe it would make the witches go away.

'My ma says that Europe copied the twelve stars for the countries from Our Lady,' he said.

I looked at him. 'Why?'

'Because we're in a big community. We can share butter and everything. That's what the stars are for.'

I giggled and he looked at me, frowning. He had a white dress on.

'What's that dress for?' I asked.

He went red and his hands pulled at it. His nails were all bitten. Bitten to the quick was what my Aunty Sheila said about mine until I gave up biting them.

'It's like a man's nightdress. It's stupid and I can't wait to get out of here to take it off.'

'What's your name?'

31

'John Paul.'

'You've the same name as the Pope.'

He shrugged, wiggling his toes. Those nails weren't bitten to the quick. They were just dirty looking.

'Dirk.' I held out my hand and bowed my head.

He just stood there. Footsteps were nearing.

'Pray,' he said. 'On your knees, Dick.'

And we both knelt down in front of the statue. I looked at her. Our Lady of Europe.

'Boys,' a lady's voice said, but not a cross voice. It was like it was hard for her to speak.

'Sister,' John Paul said, 'I'm just helping him pray to Our Lady that his operation is okay. We're praying that she'll help the doctors fix him like they fixed me. That's why I'm going home in the morning.'

'I see. You boys are praying. That statue is from Lourdes in France. I brought it back myself. And beside her is the Infant of Prague. But of course you knew that already.'

I thought that the way she was looking at us maybe she didn't believe us. But then the lines around her mouth sort of curved a bit, like a smile trying to get out of her face. I nodded. 'I am very afraid.'

'You will *fix* him, won't you, Sister?'

'That's what we're here for,' she said, letting the smile through. 'Now, then.'

Now then.

'Now, back into bed with you. You need to get your sleep.'

'Okay,' we said together and we ran up the corridor.

And as we ran up the corridor it seemed even longer and filled with more sparkles than when we'd run down it.

A Taste of Heaven

His Dracula outfit for Halloween hung on a hook at the back of his door, waiting for him. We'd such fun making the cloak out of an old black slip of mine that had become misshapen with age. I'd bought face paints and false teeth in Hector Grey's. He was going to be a *wow* as my mother would have said. I decided to leave the bed as he'd left it: khaki green sheets under and over, followed by a dusty pink wool blanket, and topped off with the bedspread I'd knitted when he was in my belly. His navy cotton pyjamas were folded on top of his pillow and crowned by Ted, his favourite teddy. Ted's right arm was worn and thin at the joint and his left ear (the one Dirk used to rub between his forefinger and thumb) was threadbare. I stayed a minute, maybe two, staring at Ted. I wanted to pick him up and cuddle him, taking in Dirk's smell, willing him to appear at the door. But I was afraid. I was afraid to touch anything and left the room.

Why would somebody abduct my son?

There would be no motive and nothing to be gained from taking him. There was no easy money to be had and besides, the good money was to be made in kidnapping horses – the hunt was on for Shergar who had been kidnapped in Kildare.

Why would somebody abduct my son?

But that wasn't the question asked.

The question that was asked was why would a nine-year-old boy run away? Why would he run away from a warm and loving home in leafy south county Dublin? What was it in his family life that *made* him run away?

And the do-gooders, their fingers dirty with the ugliness of the moral high ground, would point directly at me, the mother. The mother who dared step outside the conversations about how to keep school uniforms clean and the wonders of Mr Sheen polish. Although the EEC had pushed the government into finally lifting the ban on married women working, via two acts in '74 and '77, the mindset that believed women should not be married and in paid employment still lingered on. For the past three years I'd been teaching German in the local community centre Monday and Wednesday mornings and from six to nine on a Tuesday evening. I couldn't bear to sit and crochet one more bonnet for the infants in Africa with the ladies' club. But I was always there at the school gate, Dirk's *Beano* in my hand, waiting.

I was always there.

I was always there for him, except at the moment when he disappeared, when he didn't make the few steps to our front door. I ran my hands through my hair. I scratched the side of my nose. I rubbed my belly. I had carried this child for nine months, nursed him for ten, surely the connection would be strong enough for me to sense when he was in danger? Surely I would have felt something? Had I really no instinct at all?

I shuddered as I realised I had used the past tense and already pronounced him *gone*. I couldn't catch my breath. *I am always there for my Dirk*. And all that my darling Sepp could say in answer to my desperate repetitive cries was that he knew. He knew I was always there for Dirk. It felt like when the detested grandfather clock from Mother's house stopped ticking and I found the silence suddenly unbearable; when Sheila, my rock of a sister had trained herself to get used to the tinnitus after her accident and without warning it stopped. We had forgotten the minor miracles and were pulled out of the whirlwind of life as we knew it.

Acknowledging that our nine-year-old son, Dirk, was missing that Friday seemed to signal the beginning of the end.

The Gardaí had asked us for recent photographs to give out to those involved in the search. Sepp just stood looking out the window of our bedroom, the curtains not yet drawn, and the main light on.

'Come on,' I cajoled, 'we have to do this whether we like it or not.'

'Why didn't you just collect him from Johnston's house?'

'Why? Because he's nine years old. I haven't collected him

from Johnston's house – which we can almost see from our bloody front door – for the last two years. Christ Almighty! Did you expect me to *know* he was going to disappear! What sort of stupid thing is that to say?'

'Dirk is my light, the one who shows me how wonderful my life is.'

He looked old, then, older than his almost-fifty years, his accent stronger, his collectedness slipping. I looked at him, thinking that if Dirk were Sepp's *light,* who was he to me? I thought back to the first time I walked him to school; my *Oskie,* my baby Oscar Wilde. Each time I thought he was so big, when I looked back from a different vantage point, he was small, vulnerable; my responsibility. And now. I turned back to the job in hand, my head beginning to pound, and selected five photographs from Dirk's old shoebox (he was a size five now; the box was for a size one). I couldn't allow myself to dwell on the possibilities. One of the photographs had been taken on his last birthday, blowing out his birthday cake candles, his cake in the shape of a guitar. And two were taken last St Patrick's Day, our family tradition of a Paddy's Day snap. We really should have framed some of these; Sepp and Dirk facing each other, nose to nose; Dirk sandwiched between me and Sepp. I fingered the corner of that one, the gap of his absence ever widening. We only framed the first one we took on Paddy's Day, after Dirk had started school.

I remembered how Sepp carried his Pentax camera diagonally across his chest and walked a step or two ahead of me. How I clutched Dirk's hand, terrified he would willingly take off into the crowd. I remembered nearly giving myself a hernia lifting him onto my shoulders to see a float full of clowns and jugglers which was followed by a huge triage of baton-swinging, leg-kicking Americans dressed in red, white and blue with shamrocks over their chests, their shiny skin and impossibly high ponytails and equally high skirts lost on the children.

Even though a light misty rain had begun to fall, it was practically suffocating standing at the front of the crowd, the pressure of the push coming from behind, the knock of children's swinging legs perched on parents' shoulders. Dirk loved it. Sepp had taken the photo before I was ready and in it I had an unhappy, pained look on my face, which itself was strained with him supporting his plump body by pulling at the sides of my head. Though Dirk's face was filled with a tiny-toothed grin, his eyes were strangely expressionless, wide and blue, framed by a single curl of lush black hair resting auspiciously on his forehead. The palpitations started and I kept thinking somebody somewhere was telling the story of what was happening to us as a joke in bad taste. And the tears came. And became sobs.

I grabbed Ted from Dirk's bed. It made no difference whether I left things as they were or not. Dirk was gone. I breathed in his smell, petting Ted's head.

*

'Go on,' they said, like we were real friends or we were all in a play together, 'if you drink it quickly you'll feel the buzz. Go on.'

It was like I couldn't breathe. There we were in a graveyard and her in her grotto around the corner not able to see us but just there, always there, her blue eyes like magnets.

Joan of Arc had visions. They were given to her as gift, that's what she said. And a taste of heaven was being given to me; it was the blue Lady who led me to the visions.

The boys. I stared. They were older than me. One in a dark navy top with the hood pulled up. The other with an earring in his nose and his hair – orange, green, spiked. He looked cold but he still smiled. I liked him. That's what I wanted, I thought. A vision. I held my hand out; it was shaking.

The boy in the hood frowned. 'Well? Are you going to drink some or not?'

I thought of the warmth of the sun and how it shone on the gold of her crown. I took the plastic bottle and drank like I was in the desert, parched. They clapped when I let out a burp. They slapped me on the back.

'Welcome to the club.'

A gentle warmth passed over my eyelids, like butterflies' wings. I giggled and when I looked back at her I saw that her dress was grey. I bent down to touch the ground in front of the headstone. It was spinning. They were laughing. And then I felt the clay. I clawed at it like a dog or a fox or something that claws or digs and it was in my nails and I tasted it and drank some more and giggled and it was like I could feel everything. I was part of this, this muck, this grass, this liquid. These strange boys were feeding me like I was their pet; I belonged to them.

'Hey,' the hooded guy said.

I looked at him.

'We're heading, like,' the spiky-haired one said.

'Okay,' I replied. I looked at my fingers like they weren't mine anymore.

'Not far. We're just going over there to sit down a while.'

'Right.'

'Are you okay? Will you be okay?'

They looked at each other. Then they just shrugged their shoulders.

'I'm okay,' I said.

*

From keeping ourselves to ourselves, the whole neighbourhood now knew us and knew of Dirk. They nodded, serious looks on their faces as they drew their children closer to them, as if disappearing was contagious.

'Do you know,' I said to Sepp, a sudden surge of hope as we circled near the Johnstons' house for the third time. 'We should go for a meal to celebrate, when we find him, treat ourselves. What about Nico's in town? We could order spaghetti Bolognese, garlic bread, the whole shebang, and big pieces of Black Forest gateau, even a glass of wine.'

Sepp looked at me, his face full of accusation. 'Dirk,' he began, and stopped. Then, 'Dirk,' he repeated and shook his head, pressing the bridge of his nose with his fingers. 'I mean, that Garda, what a waste of time. And this?'

'Or not,' I said, feeling nervous, my headache full-blown.

37

There was a possibility, of course, that we wouldn't find him.

Jackie Johnston was unable to shed any light; they had played out in the garden with their hats and coats on, come back inside for a drink of milk and some biscuits. They'd then gone upstairs to Paul's room to play Pac-Man. Sepp wanted to know what they had played in the garden. Paul had walked Dirk to the corner – as agreed with me – waved goodbye and was back, at home, with her about two or three minutes later.

We walked away from her house in silence, Sepp scraping his shoes against the pavement. I stopped, feeling the adrenalin rush through me suddenly. 'Dirk once told me that the older boys play hide-and-seek around the church grounds. Maybe he did say goodbye to Paul but then hooked up with some of the other boys? Or maybe Jackie *thought* they played in the garden but they had, in fact, played with the older boys?'

'He knows not to go anywhere without telling you,' he reminded me. 'You know how he likes his home comforts,' he said, his voice flat. 'He wouldn't just run away for nothing.'

'Let's go.'

Sepp looked at me. 'Where? It's too late, Mary. He's gone.' Tears rolled down his face. He started sobbing. 'I've a book I bought him, *The Little Prince*. I should have given it to him instead of saving it for a special occasion. My little prince.'

'Sepp,' I shouted. 'Stop it. We *will* find him. We're going to the church.'

*

The sun catches me.

Blinded, I disappear inside the blue of her eyes, feeling the smile inside, hearing the lull of the 'shh'.

The blue Lady is gentle like other mothers. Other mothers who smile all the time. Who pet your hair. Other mothers who *believe*.

Climbing over the stone wall, I cut the side of my hand on the granite stone, its sparkles like happiness. Jagged little blood drops in the sun. I squeeze it, hold my hand up so she'll see the blood.

I am like her Son: my hands have holes. My palms bleed like his.

I tell her about the witches who hide in the wardrobe in my room. Sometimes they laugh at me. Other times they cry quietly because they have nobody to talk to.

She smiles, telling me she is here, always here.

I put my coat on the ground and sit on it. It's dark now but still.

Still I can see the blue of her eyes.

Why, I ask. Why are you so gentle? Why can't other mothers be gentle?

And then she smiles. She smiles and her lips don't move but I hear her voice. Sweet, like a robin's chirrup.

I am beautiful, she says, *because I love. You must love to be beautiful.*

I think of Aunty Sheila. She isn't really beautiful even though she wears scarves with pretty colours. Is it because she doesn't love anyone special? Or is it because she carries sadness in a bucket with her, like *Vati* says?

My mammy is beautiful. When I hug her she's soft. I know sometimes she doesn't love me, the way she looks at me, like I've done something really wrong. But I don't know what. Or how to make things better again. Mammy doesn't believe in heaven.

Heaven, she says, *is a large space. It is a light that doesn't exist on earth. Everyone wears the same clothes. All grey. It is a large space of nothing.*

Is that why Mammy doesn't believe? She can't look at lights because of her headaches. Is that why she can't see the happiness?

Our Lady smiles and I see a glimmer in her eyes.

Some people, she says, her gentle voice making me feel sleepy, *are not able to believe because they cannot see. But you are not like that, are you, Dirk?*

Dirk.

She tells me to wake up and go somewhere warm. I jump up, grab my coat. My head hurts and I feel sick. I look at her. She's dark now. *Now then.* Grey. Maybe she's gone back to heaven.

39

She doesn't have the gold stars around her anymore. She's changed her clothes, somehow, and has a look of curiosity about her. My Aunty Sheila says that curiosity killed the cat. I look at her eyes again, waiting for something but she just has that look in them. She's waiting for me to do the talking, like *Vati* says to me about Mammy.

I'm curious, Our Lady, I say. I'm curious as to how you transform yourself.

And then, like a flash, I remember that the Prague one wasn't here, she was the one in the hospital and that I was dreaming of the hospital, about me and John Paul running in our dirty feet down the black corridor with Our Lady watching us and the nurse saying *now then*.

She's waiting for me to say something with meaning. I run into the church. Maybe the Prague one is in there.

I listen to the sound of my bare feet on the tiles on the floor. Slap. Slap. Slap. I can't remember where I've put my runners. I feel so tired.

A man's voice calls.

'Hello?'

But I don't answer because I don't have time now. I have to get to the top of the stairs. I'd said I'd look out the window at her from up on high; she'd said God was up on high, so I had to get to the highest bit.

I get to the top of the stairs. They're in a circle, a spiral, like those stones at Newgrange, all in circles, like the story of life itself, the salmon of knowledge where it goes then comes back again, like all knowledge.

I get to the top and it looks like the floor is sparkling and I feel woozy and I remember, suddenly, how sick I was after my operation, how I just vomited without stopping and it came out, red blood came out of my mouth and I cried I was so afraid of the blood. There was snot from my nose and more blood. I remember the red lemonade they made me drink and how it hurt my throat so badly that I cried. And I cried even more when Aunty Sheila brought me a brand new set of fancy markers and a pad full of crisp white paper. I felt so sick I couldn't ever imagine being strong enough to draw or colour or

40

even hold the drawing pad.

Now I'm getting sick.

Underneath the organ. I cover the pedals in it but this time it isn't blood, it's beige. Yes, this time it isn't camel brown, or a colour that's *in*, it's beige-gold liquid, like the drink they'd given me. I vomit and it drips like gooey stuff off the pedals onto the floor. I lay my head down beside the pedals and watch it drip, drip, drip.

*

It was now more than six hours since I had seen him and almost four since he was last seen by Paul at the top of the road. I kept thinking that maybe I would be burying my son next week. If he was found dead. If he was found at all. There was a black dress in the back of the wardrobe that I hadn't worn in ages, which would do for the funeral. He wouldn't be small enough for a child's coffin, yet not big enough for an adult-sized coffin. Or did they make them to fit people, I wondered? Did coffins just come in specific child or adult, pine or oak? Mahogany would suit Dirk, I decided. Solid, beautiful, timeless yet traditional.

'What's wrong with these parents, letting children wander around like hooligans?' Sepp said bitterly as we passed two drunken teenagers huddled behind a giant Angel Gabriel with their flagons of cheap cider. I ran after them as they scrambled to their feet, eager to escape.

'Wait,' I called, my voice high-pitched, suddenly hopeful. They could be Dirk in a few years' time, empty, aimless. 'Please wait. We're looking for a nine-year-old boy. Dark curly hair, tall, broad-shouldered. Have you seen him?'

They stopped walking.

'Curly hair?' the one with the spiked hair said. 'Yeah, there was a boy with curly hair around here. He was looking for drink.'

'We told him to go home,' the one with a hooded top on put in, a little too quickly.

'What time was this?' Sepp stepped forward, his face flushed.

'It's my boy. He's been missing for hours.'

'Jesus Christ. It's freezing out here. He didn't have a coat on. He kept singing that stupid Culture Club song.' The boy held up an imaginary microphone. '*Do You Really Want to Hurt Me?*' He rolled his eyes. 'I mean, who the fuck listens to that stuff?'

'When did you see him?' Sepp was shaking the first one by the shoulders.

'Hang on, Mister. Hang on. No need to get all aggressive, like.'

Sepp stepped back. 'Sorry. He's only nine.'

'It was around an hour or so ago, maybe more. He said he had no home to go to any more.'

They started laughing. 'I mean he said that the lady in the grey dress had told him to come here, to find… '

'Find what?'

'He had to find true… '

They were hysterical now.

'Happiness.'

*

Mammy's voice, far away. I cough. I close my eyes again and think Our Lady is cold out there on her own. I need to find her. I need to ask her about the sparkles on the floor in the hospital, if she put them there especially for me. I think she did. Deep down I *know* she did. My throat hurts and my head is sore. Am I beautiful enough to love? Or is it that I have to love to be beautiful? I'm not sure if she believed me when I told her there were witches in my room. And demons, too. She never said anything when I told her about my room. But then after a few minutes she told me again that she's here, always here for me.

I hear footsteps downstairs and voices. I giggle and I don't feel sick any more. I draw my knees up under my chin and start counting.

*

Sepp shook his head and scuffed his shoes back and forth on

42

the ground, first one then the other. I took a deep breath and went in alone. The heels of my shoes echoed off the marble floor, the vastness of the empty church seeming larger. I rubbed my hands together.

'It's cold isn't it?' A voice which I assumed to be Father Connolly's came from the door I'd just walked through. He was tall and graceful, like an athlete, I thought. He would be bald in a few years and he'd swept the bit of hair he still had across his head.

'Yes, I'm looking for a boy of nine, lost,' I said, not sure if the sudden inner warmth I was feeling was a sign that something good would come out of this visit, or if it just brought back memories of being at church with my grandmother. 'Dirk Horn,' I added.

'Garda Gleeson was on to me,' Father Connolly said.

The last time I'd been in a church was when Dirk made his First Holy Communion. We'd dressed him – like all the parents dressed their sons – like a miniature man. His suit was a dove grey and he wore a white shirt with a white knitted tie. His shoes were a little large for him but he loved how they shone. 'I can see my face in them,' he kept repeating over and over, bending down trying to see his reflection without losing his balance. Any of the true religious significance was lost on him amid the excitement and buzz of the lead up to the day and the day itself. His prayer book had a thick cream vinyl cover, which he thought was marble, with a gold cross in the centre of it. He used to tell me the cross was speaking to him, telling him how special he was.

'Mary,' Father Connolly said, reaching out to take my hand, 'I know you and your husband don't practise but I will help you find Dirk because all children are God's children. Whether they go to Mass or not. Or have any religion at all. They should, of course, but – '

' – he used to bring a statue of the Child of Prague to bed with him, to protect him from the witches, he said.'

'Your son is special. He's led you to the right place.'

I shivered and strained my head back, looking up at the dark wooden beams above, my eyes drawn towards flashes of blues and reds coming from the stained-glass windows. I remembered how Dirk had asked me why those people were so mean to Jesus and why didn't his mammy take him home? I took a deep breath and walked towards the confessional boxes with their luxurious velvet curtains, the very ones Dirk had asked if he could have for his room. I pulled the curtains back, slowly, hoping he'd be sitting there, hands joined in prayer, eyes shut, his voice in a whisper, hearing the imaginary confession of a lost soul. A soul that mirrored his own. Empty space and the scent of highly polished wood greeted me. We looked behind the granite holy water stands; nothing. You could see under the seats – there was nothing there either. The church was deserted.

'I thought I heard footsteps earlier,' Father Connolly ventured, 'but when I called out nobody answered.'

I looked at him. Suddenly I felt hatred for this man, childless, bereft of possessions and love but still the keeper of the mysteries my son so desperately wanted to be part of. He looked upwards. A noise, like a scraping or a tapping came from the direction of the top left corner of the church. I walked towards the sound. It came again. Father Connolly followed behind.

'Dirk?' I shouted. My voice sounded like nothing I had ever heard. It was a screech. A howl. A scream. 'Dirk baby? Oskie? My Oskie?' I was running. I was running up the left-hand aisle, my shoes clattering on the marble. I was watching myself, watching myself and I was running, my eyes wild, searching. The direction of the noise changed; it seemed to come from above us now. The noise was definitely coming from above us. It stopped. And then. A giggle.

'Dirk!' I screamed. I ran back down the aisle. 'Where are you?' My voice angry, I climbed the stairs to the organ.

The door of the church creaked open below and I could hear Sepp running through the church, taking the steep steps two at a time.

Another giggle. But I couldn't see anything. My own breathing was heavy and loud.

'Dirk, come out, now.' Father Connolly, the voice of authority. He shone his torch around.

'You found me!'

Dirk came out from under the organ with a tiny statue of the Child of Prague in his hand, his cheeks roaring red, eyes glassy.

'Three hundred and twenty-seven,' he said.

I grabbed him, buried my face in his neck as Sepp reached the top of the stairs. The stench of alcohol hit me. I took a deep breath. There was dried vomit in his hair. I wiped my tears away with the back of my hand.

'Oh God. You're here. You're *here*. Dirk.'

I handed Dirk to Sepp like he was a prize we'd won. We'd deal with the drinking later. Sepp was sniffling, wiping the tears with the back of his suede gloves. He took him in his arms.

'You're here, Dirk, you're here,' he said.

'I was here all the time,' Dirk replied, wiggling out from Sepp's embrace, a bewildered look on his face. He clutched the statue tightly with both hands.

'But Dirk, we didn't know you were here.'

'I was digging, just a little, and the ground… ' He held out his hands, muck encased in his fingernails, dried blood on his left palm. The zip on his trousers was undone. His feet were bare.

'Dirk.'

'It was dirty and Our Lady, showed me how to be beautiful, how to love.' Dirk looked away.

I frowned, taking a deep breath.

'Now, child,' Father Connolly said, an edge to his voice, 'what have you been doing?'

Dirk rubbed his eyes, sleepily yawning as Sepp slowly lifted him inside his coat.

'I was here all the time,' Dirk muttered, his eyelids fluttering, as if shielding themselves from a bright light.

*

I feel so sleepy and as *Vati* lifts me up I look at Mammy's eyes. A line of light from the torch the priest is holding shines on her eyes and then they're blue, not brown, but blue like Our Lady's eyes.

45

And she's smiling at me, telling me she's there for me and I'm smiling back. And warmth is spreading and I think that we are going to heaven.

We are all beautiful now.

We are all beautiful now.

Tara's Hotel

There are things we're told in hushed tones. Nuggets of gold which turn out to be worthless. It was an extraordinary week of endings and beginnings, the week Tara told me all about it. I was agog. Or, more accurately, morally astounded.

Until that day over a cup of Earl Grey tea in Bewley's Café on Westmorland Street, I had thought that good was a term like nice. We all want to be thought of as good or nice but not necessarily be described that way. Tara, not only thought of as nice, was quite often described as good. A good friend, a good person. She always did the right thing, said just what was needed in precisely the right tone. But as my Earl Grey went cold, I listened to the details (too much if the truth be told) of how her lover took her to a hotel on the Dublin-Sligo road and wooed her. That was actually the word she used.

'He wooed me,' she said and screamed like a schoolgirl.

'Tara,' I said, uncomfortable with this revelation, 'nobody *woos* a woman of twenty-nine.'

She crossed her thin, perfectly shaped arms. 'Well,' she said, 'I have been wooed, I've felt it and I know for a fact that you have not.'

You see, as well as being good, Tara was also sharp. She knew how to hurt as much as to help. Here was a woman who had only worn Vaseline with her full pillar-box red lips. He was German. They'd met at a conference.

'He had these eyes. It sounds trite but they were like magnets. I stayed for after-dinner drinks. Can you believe it? I even smoked a cigar.'

'Some healthcare conference,' I muttered.

I was jealous, I had to admit it. Trying to control a bunch of teenagers and ram the history of our godforsaken country down their throats so that they could finish school and go on the dole queue or head off to the building sites in England had never held any glamour. The possibility of meeting people and drinking – being paid to enjoy – sat before me, challenging.

'Besides all of this,' Tara's tone was somewhat triumphant, 'I might get a job out of it. I won't just be a nurse. I could be an actual representative in a pharmaceutical company. Think about it. I could be with him and go on all these trips. They even have conferences in places like the Canaries or San Marino. Oh.' She clasped her hands. 'I can just picture it.'

There was a dress of mine which kept trying to escape out of my wardrobe. I'd worn it only once. It'd peek out, midnight blue caught in the doors, and I thought then that I'd go with her, for company, and wear it in San Marino. I'd never seen her look so damned radiant. Once I'd pictured myself in that dress – a man of my own on my arm, beige slacks, tanned, slicked back hair – I could see where she was coming from.

She twirled her straight hair around her index finger before continuing.

'Mr and Mrs Pratt,' he'd said, and produced a gold credit card. His wedding ring caught the light and she felt bad, she said, but the excitement quickly took over the guilt. As soon as they were in the lift he pushed her against the mirror and kissed her. 'Tara,' he said with each breath. As she told me the story she flushed.

'What did you say to him?' I wanted to hear that she said something outrageous, shocking. Or that she'd refused him, that she'd told him she couldn't and wouldn't join in this charade of lust.

'Nothing.' She looked surprised. 'I just kept kissing and then before I realised it we were out of the lift and in Room 159 and he had thrown his briefcase with a bang on the floor and I'd kicked off my shoes and I was wiggling out of my skirt like I'd done this a thousand times.'

'You knew.' I gritted my teeth. The good girl knew.

'Of course. Jesus, Eve, you don't go to a hotel bedroom to play snakes and ladders.' She took a breath, composed herself. 'We didn't even make it to the bed.' She blushed, giggling. 'I mean we went from the bed to the floor and then to – '

' – okay I get the picture.'

We ordered more tea and cherry buns. I watched her pick the icing off hers. She picked the flesh of the bun with nimble fingers, eating soundlessly. Curious that silence and control, I thought. As I watched her she beamed at me then bit the side of her lip. Some of her new lipstick rubbed off on her teeth. I almost reached across to wipe her teeth clean.

'Can you believe it?' she asked.

'I guess not.'

*

I took to going to hotels myself, then. Just to see what the bedrooms were like. The distance from the bed to the floor, for example. It's amazing how many beds are so bloody high off the ground you'd wonder about the percentage of injuries people sustain in hotel bedrooms or how many of them sue. How many feet from the bed to the bathroom, say, or an armchair (do people do it sitting?) or the door, for example.

'I'm thinking,' I'd say to the receptionist. 'I'm thinking of bringing my husband for a surprise weekend and I'd like to see your suite if it's free.'

Or sometimes I'd say I was engaged and the ring was being resized and I was thinking of having the wedding and could I visit the honeymoon suite or the bridal suite. And they'd look at me, momentarily surprised, but then they'd take me seriously and pull out all the stops. Once – to be truthful, a few times – I got a free lunch and a glass of half-decent wine. I made a few sketches of the layout of the rooms – they were amazingly similar – and a genuine interest in the architecture of the hotels was sparked. I must say, for a grand entrance (I was picturing myself, of course, with my man on my arm, in my midnight blue dress) I concluded that you couldn't beat The Gresham on Dublin's O'Connell Street. Think Scarlett O'Hara, polished pointy nails, plush carpets, the real chandeliers. Though perhaps it was nothing to do with the décor and all to do with the sense of history.

I would bring it into class, I decided, just do a bit on how O'Connell Street looked in, let's say, April 1916. The

49

receptionist even said she'd try and dig out some old guest books for me, or records they might have of menus. She kindly suggested that next time I try the National Library's historical archives. There were teams, she said, teams of people working on cataloguing all sorts of interesting documents for historians like me. I almost corrected her by saying I wasn't actually an historian but then, I thought, no, it suited me, the tag of historian as much as adulterer suited Tara.

I asked Tara if he moved their liaisons around, you know, in case they were seen.

'No,' she said, pint in hand in Bruxelles just off Grafton Street, our favourite place, 'we have one hotel and our room 159 – it works.'

'But' – I just wanted to know – 'how often do you meet these days?'

She looked at me strangely as she confessed that it had turned into a fortnightly thing, on a Thursday. They'd have dinner in the hotel, a bottle of wine and then stay the night.

Ah, I thought. So it had progressed. I could see the difference in her eyes. She wore more make-up, her brown eyes highlighted with peacock blue eye-shadow to match her wide patent belt and boxed jacket. Her nails were squared with a French polish. She had a choppy fringe cut into her hair, long bits at the back. A bit like Bananarama you could say. She was fashionable. She talked of Leeson Street clubs and name dropped brands of wine I'd never heard of. She walked with a swagger I'd not seen before.

The thing was. The thing was that all of these changes suited her. She wasn't turning into Tara-the-arch-bitch. She was still Tara-good-old-Tara and the truth was I was beginning to hate her. Yes. I began to hate the girl I had grown up next door to (or maybe I had hated her all along and just had not acknowledged it).

Tara Jenkins, once upon a time *my* girl next door.

*

I decided to park the trip to the National Library archives and instead saved my money and energy until I had enough of both to book room 160 on Thursday 13th September.

I have to say, I was very excited about it all. What I was worried about though, was the timing. I hadn't figured out what explanation I would give if we happened to bump into each other. I guess you could say I'm a curious sort of neighbour. It stems from when me and Tara used to send each other messages out the bathroom window with our torches, you know the way kids do that. It was more than just kids' play, though. It was an experience Tara and I shared together.

The plan was I'd get to the hotel, check in, and wait. I'd get a toasted cheese sandwich and a tea from room service and watch, God, I don't know, Magnum or The A-Team or who knew, even The Muppets would have done it. I'd have the TV on low or even mute to be sure I heard them come in next door. It was like a little holiday. A break from my little bedsit – nice though it was – and a chance to stretch out on a large bed, flick through MTV and have food brought to me by smartly-dressed room service people.

In the room there was an armchair: velvet, pale beige almost white, with large invasions of brown flowers on it. I touched it, stroked it and thought of her, next door, probably comparing the feel of the velvet to her lover's hair, newly cut. I puffed up the pillows and lay them on top of each other, like a tower. I plonked myself on the fluffy mess. The Cars were on MTV followed by Michael Jackson. I sang along and then lowered the sound.

Her laughter. It was more high-pitched than I remembered it but I put that down to her being excited. I wondered if he'd done his lift thing, you know, just to get her all fired up. I could hear her footsteps and she was even humming a song. It sounded like that Doors song, *Light My Fire*. I almost laughed. I'd missed her going into the room.

I could hear the Angelus bells ringing out through her TV. I sat on the bed then stood up again. I pressed my ear to the wall but could hear nothing except for the TV. So I switched channels on the one in my room. We were never particularly religious in my house, growing up, I mean, to the extent that I didn't know what prayers to be saying with the Angelus bells ringing. I said two Hail Marys that evening. One for me: that I might find lasting happiness or a sudden rush of love, and one for Tara: that she might keep what she had already found. I felt better afterwards; it was like a relief, almost, like the feeling you get when you make your First Confession as a kid, like that Frank O'Connor story – you're all full of confusion and guilt and then it's gone, in a flash, you do the right thing in the sing-song of words muttered in prayer.

I ordered my tea and ate it, cross-legged on the bed, flicking the crumbs with my feet. I wasn't the one who had to hoover the room. I considered going to the bar. Maybe there would be someone to talk to, to liaise with, to embrace. I finished my sandwich and flicked through the stations again. It was hard to decide what to watch. In the end I settled on that guy with large glasses on MTV chatting on about some competition that I knew half my students would enter. I considered entering it myself: I wouldn't have minded winning a trip to New York, but sure I was too old and who would I bring?

I'd had enough entertainment. I pressed the little red button on the right-hand side of the remote control. There wasn't a sound from next door. I counted the crumbs on my bed. With a magnificent sweep of my hand they went onto the floor just as I heard a man's voice.

'Tara, Tara.'

And then her laughter, not as high-pitched now, a deeper, throatier laugh.

I stood to the side of the bed. I thought about the sounds I might make if I was with this Sepp Horn. This man with such a strange name. It didn't roll off the tongue like you'd imagine a lover's name should.

I tried to imagine how he might look at me. An eye filled with lust or mischief. I had Tara's disjointed descriptions of his tall frame, his delicate hands with piano fingers. How would it feel as those fingers played their way across, let's say, my thigh? Would I laugh, like her? Or would I be conscious of nothing but the movement of my skin against his? Or the sound of my body on his as I slid myself across him and his fingers curled

52

themselves around my bare back?

I stood and looked at myself in the full-length mirror as I slowly undressed, letting my clothes fall in a contrived heap around my broad, ghost-like feet. I'd packed my midnight blue dress in the bag. I'd thought to myself *just in case*. I took it out and held it against my body. Her laughter had stopped. The sound of my furious breathing filled the silence. In the light of the hotel room, my face in the mirror was red; an angry, shameful look across it, like it wasn't mine. I stuffed the dress back in the bag, punching it down so that it would lie, unused. I took a whiskey from the mini-bar and drank it in one go.

There was a beat against the wall. One. Two. Three. And again. I knelt on the bed and pressed my palms to the wall, flexing my fingers in time to the snippets of their lovemaking. I began rocking – Eve and Tara, I whispered. How we used to imagine we were the last two on earth as we shone the washed out light of our torches out the windows. Our friendship faded, for a while, and then grew bright again with freedom and dance and drink. And love, of course.

But now it was Tara and Sepp. Tara and Sepp. And Eve. Sometimes Eve as a standby. I no longer belonged in the same sentence as Tara. I pressed my palms flat against the wall and looked at the goose bumps on the skin of my thighs. And it dawned on me with such a wave of resignation, that you're always an addendum if you have to be added onto something.

I must have drifted off to sleep because I could hear, then, the sound of a shower, or water in a bath going. I lay there listening to the water. Somebody was cleaning themselves, refreshing the scent on their skin. I'd no choice myself, then, but to take a shower, rid myself of the traces of being a teacher. I deliberately put the water on hot. The jets almost burned me but being able to take a shower after ten at night was beyond a luxury. It was something, simply, that I'd not had the opportunity to do until then.

I dried myself slowly and then used up all the body lotion from the tiny bottle. It smelled like lilac. Reminiscent of the smell that would linger in my grandmother's room after she'd gone to powder her nose before Mass. The flow of water had stopped next door too. There was silence. No giggles or sighs or whispers. I squashed the little empty bottle under my bare foot thinking that maybe the scent of lilac did not have to mean old-fashioned. I was pampering myself, that was all.

Despite my little nap, I fell asleep the minute my head hit the pillow. I dreamt of my grandfather's funeral and how I held my grandmother's hand in mine. And her hand smelled of damp earth. Not a trace of lilac.

*

The next morning as I strolled down the stairs for breakfast, I decided that I would carry on as normal. That is, pretend to myself that I had somehow discovered their joy, partaken in it by proxy and was now a woman with a mission accomplished.

The breakfast room was long and consisted of several round tables running through it with four alcoves in the corners. She was in the corner, by the window. Tara. Her hair perfectly combed; a bottle of spray holding it in place, probably. Her lips were bare, though, maybe, I thought, she had licked them clean. I watched her pick up her fork, her nails now lilac (I couldn't help smiling at this) and she slowly cut into a rasher. She was neat in how she ate, like a sparrow was what my mother used to say.

He came and sat down beside her. His frame was bulky but not fat; he was taller than most of the other men in the room but his head of black curls was what distinguished him. Not even his name was as memorable as his hair. As a child – she told me that he'd told her this on their second meeting – he'd had white blond hair which his mother had refused to cut until he'd wept, begging her to, at aged five. They were comfortable with each other, relaxed, casual you could even say. He'd reach across the sausages and eggs and pet her hand and she'd smile at him. He'd wipe a bit of egg yolk off the corner of her mouth. I stuffed myself. I ate a whole grapefruit, three triangles of toast and a full fry. I licked my lips like a madwoman; the tang of the grapefruit, the salt of the rashers. For that alone, the effort of the trip felt worth it.

Soon they got talking to an elderly couple beside them. They were all laughing at some joke. At one point an ageing waitress in a ridiculous French maid outfit went over to them, shook their hands and then took a seat for a few minutes. There was clasping of hands and heads thrown back like a reunion of old friends. I was furious. I guess I just couldn't believe I hadn't been seen. Maybe it was love, after all, that did not need to be seen. It was just I, the one with nothing to show off, who *wanted* to be seen.

Not bothering to drop my bag off at the flat, I went straight to work feeling utterly exhausted. I'd have to try and make it again, get the money somehow. I gave my third year class the biggest amount of homework they'd ever had to do.

'Success will be your happiness,' I shouted at them.

They looked at me strangely, like I'd just walked into class for the first day.

'Believe me,' I said, lowering my voice, 'you must succeed in whatever you do if you want to be happy.'

The bell rang and in the staff room I kept my head down, busy with my diary, working out when I might be able to go back and stay in room 160.

*

Circumstances took over, though, as so often they do. Tara's affair was only ever meant to be short-lived because Sepp Horn keeled over with a heart attack a few weeks later.

She was devastated, insisting I accompany her to the funeral.

'You really shouldn't show your face,' I tried to tell her.

'They don't know. I'm a work colleague, that's all. I'm just one of many.'

Her face looked grey when she said that and it was true. She was, in more ways than one, just one of many. I have to say the whole thing disturbed me. I was astonished at the level of grief Tara was displaying for what was really just a seven month fling. Not even enough time to procreate. And besides all of this, I had become accustomed to the experience of love a hand removed. The death affected me too.

A huge wreath had been sent on behalf of the company and, even though she'd wanted to send a card, Tara knew she couldn't. A large wreath of pink, blue and white flowers bore the company emblem and a tiny card bore the words 'Sepp Horn will be sadly missed'. Somebody had hand-written his name in the gap before the typed script. A sort of fill-in-the-blanks. Tara was furious.

At the funeral Mass we sat at the back of the church and watched as his son gave a reading. What was he? Seventeen? Eighteen? It was too hard to tell, the way his curly dark hair fell over his face. He read slowly and clearly, as if taking a test of clarity, and when he looked at the faces watching him, his face was blank. I followed his gaze to what looked like a bunch of classmates and teachers. I thought back to when my own father had died and remembered seeing only colourless faces staring back or heads upon heads of hair, eyes cast to the ground, shamed, miserable, shocked. I remember feeling as if I had been given an anaesthetic, and was somehow asleep, yet performing in an alternative reality. In some ways this boy's performance couldn't be further from the grief-stricken only son that he should have played; it was cool, too cool. I watched Tara as she stared at him stepping down the steps of the altar in what must have been a brand new suit to sit beside his mother. The other woman. He looked like Sepp. Or rather they looked like each other.

She squeezed my hand as we stood, well back from the real mourners at the grave. I swore afterwards, I could hear the noise the dry earth made as it hit the coffin. As they all walked away from the freshly dead towards the eating of unimaginative pub sandwiches and chips I felt the need to drink neat whiskeys to numb the pain. And I thought that something resembling a life would appear again. Maybe the son would study harder, the mother go to a bridge or a painting class. Maybe they'd do as I did, play Bach's *Goldberg Variations* over and over until things shifted and each note healed. I blew my nose so hard into my yellow handkerchief that it bled. I decided that I'd have to say another prayer; I'd got it back to front. It was Tara who needed lasting happiness. It was I who needed to keep what I'd already

56

found.

We went to Grogans. It was dark inside and the old worn velvet sofas comforted us with their familiarity. The usual suspects lined the high stools at the bar. We wiggled our backsides down onto the sofas. Tara gave a pathetic laugh.

'Look at me,' she said, crumpling the silk of the black dress just above her knee. 'He gave me this, a present, he gave it to me. And now he's dead.'

'I'm sorry, Tara,' I finally said. 'I'm sorry it ended this way.'

'I just thought – ' she said as her eyes welled up. 'In the hotel I just thought I saw in Tadhg and Mabel a glimpse of what Sepp and I would be like when we were older.'

'Hey,' I said, putting my arm around her.

'They were such a nice couple.' She paused to light a cigarette. 'We met them over breakfast.' She shook her head as she blew smoke rings.

'You've not lost your party trick,' I said.

'They were celebrating their wedding anniversary. They do it every year in the same hotel at the same table.'

'Why?'

'She used to work there. Imagine! She used to fold napkins, she said, in the 70s, and the woman in the French maid outfit –'

'French maid outfit?'

'Yeah, the one who joined us at the table – she used to work *with* her. Like a pretty daisy chain of connections.' She paused. 'Gas, isn't it?'

'Mad is what it is.'

'But you know what?' She stubbed out her cigarette in a grass-green glass ashtray. 'The worst bit?'

'What?'

'They were happy,' she said, 'the couple were happy with just that to look forward to every year.'

'The hotel?' My heart skipped a beat.

'A dinner and a breakfast in a hotel. Just that.' Her hand shook as she lit another cigarette.

'So simple,' I replied, swishing my drink in its heavy glass.

'Just that gave them happiness,' she said as she began to cry.

I looked at my whiskey: fine and strong and neat.

57

Go-Go Girls

'You could get good money using that, you know.'

After a particularly busy day at the library, Dirk was in Vaughan's for a few pints and a read of the latest Paul Durcan offering: *Daddy, Daddy*. He'd been enjoying the poems, smiles and frowns alternating across his face, the cloud of unknowing lifting ever so gradually. He wanted to be able to paint pictures with the gravitas of Paul's words. He wanted so much, Dirk was thinking. He wanted so much it hurt.

Dirk had seen this guy before. They'd always nodded at each other, made small talk when ordering at the bar, but had never engaged in a proper conversation. He was easily the best dressed man in the place, his shoes always shiny. You'd see a pair on him and, next thing, they'd be on a billboard somewhere, or in a magazine. You'd see a velvet jacket on him and a striped silk tie and you'd see an ad on television for that same jacket.

Dirk looked at him: his carefully arranged quiff, his one gold-hooped earring, his gaze. Why the man would strike up a conversation in the toilets was beyond him. He shifted uneasily as he finished urinating.

'I said you could get good money using that.'

'I'm not into stuff like that, thanks,' Dirk replied in as steady a voice as he could after three Guinness.

'No, professional use, you moron. Like, proper money.'

Dirk zipped his pants and washed his hands.

'Nothing dirty,' the man said, smirking. 'A fucker like you could earn up to ten grand, easy.'

Dirk took his time drying them under the dryer. It drowned out the guy's rabbiting. As he watched the man's mouth move, Dirk's mind was working overtime, repeating something it hadn't said in a long time. *Horny Boy*. His other name throughout secondary school. The dryer stopped.

'The name's Dave. Born and bred in Finglas but living round the corner with me girlfriend, Teresa. So, what's it to be, in or out, figuratively speaking.'

'It wouldn't do any harm to have a chat about it, I suppose.' Dirk spoke slowly, measuring each word. Whatever he was talking about, he thought, if there was a chance, even a slight chance that this could be the thing to stop him wanting, he'd take it.

'That's my man. Now, another one for the road? On me?'

'Dirk Horn,' Dirk said, offering his hand in a rush of confidence.

'Fuck, we don't even have to change your name, man. You're perfect for it,' Dave said, opening the door.

He caught the barman's eye, mouthed *two*. He laughed as they sat down.

'I don't know how I didn't spot you a mile off. I'm out of me familiar zone. Southsiders have their own way of behaving, you know?'

Dirk finished off his drink. 'Aha, but I'm only, strictly speaking, fifty per cent Southside.'

'With a name like yours, Dirk, I'm surprised you're even bleedin' Irish.'

'The other fifty's German. Tayto?' Dirk held out his half-eaten pack to Dave.

'Go on then. I tell you King don't have a patch on your old Tayto, do they?' He nodded his thanks to the barman for the pints. 'Sure it's like the difference between bloody Hershey's and Cadbury's. No competition. None at all.'

'My mother prefers King, though,' said Dirk.

'Well, she's got to be in a fucking minority of one then,' said Dave. 'I mean, you just can't get that same taste from any other crisp.' He smacked his lips. 'And that, combined with a smooth Guinness. Ahhh. A man's heaven.' He paused. 'Alongside other forms of entertainment of course, if you get my drift.'

Dirk smiled.

Dave brushed stray hairs from his navy velvet coat. 'I love Elvis, me, love him. Been to Graceland every year for the last – I don't know how many years, but years and bleedin' years.

59

Love the place. How about you? You a fan of the King?'

'Aha. The quiff.'

'That's not an Elvis quiff, that's a Mozza quiff.'

'Mozza?'

'Fuck off, would you? Don't say you haven't heard of the *Moz*?'

Dirk shook his head. 'Can't say I have, Dave. Not really into music myself.'

'Not into Morrissey – music, for fuck's sake, you have to be into music living here! Thin Lizzy, U2, The Rolling Stones… the list goes on, man.'

Dirk shook his head again. 'Nope. Not into music, not into GAA, not into – '

'Not even the football? Come on. Aren't you even thinking of Italy?'

Dirk shook his head.

'World Cup? Well what are you into then?'

'Books. I'm a librarian.' Dirk held up his book.

'Poetry? Ah, Jaysus. We'll have that knocked out of you in no time, my man. No time. Once you start in this business books'll be for beggars.'

'So… are *you* long in the business, like?' Dirk swallowed, his throat suddenly dry.

Dave twirled his earring around, his hand brushing against his sandy hair. He grinned at Dirk. He burst out laughing. 'Got you, didn't I? Got you good and well, my man.'

'What?'

'You know I've been watching you and I didn't think you'd fall for it but you did. Right for it. Hook, line and fucking sinker.'

'Serious?' Dirk bit the side of his cheek as he finished his crisps.

Dave still grinned. 'I'm sort of shy, me. That's why I'm an actor, trying it out on you. Mind you, I'm resting right now.'

Dirk shook his head and, despite himself, smiled.

'But come on, man, you've got to admit, you could be in the business if you wanted.'

Just over six months later, an almost twenty-year-old Dirk wearing freshly pressed pale blue jeans, and an almost thirty-year-old Dave in tight leopard print trousers cycled side-by-side on the Terenure Road into Dublin.

Dave, short, sandy-haired and on the verge of chubbiness wobbled on a high-Nelly bike.

'Let me level with you. I've known you now a few months, nearly seven actually, and it's time to tell you about my list. I've got a notebook filled with *fuckers I have known* and if you end up on that list... '

'What do you mean if I end up on that list? I can only end up on that list if you put me on it, you idiot.' Dirk laughed to himself. This was why he'd abandoned his quiet readings and pints in the pub. The ad-hoc-ness of it all with Dave; the sheer silliness; fun for the hell of it.

'Obviously. Obviously. But if you do happen to fucking double cross me, you're in big trouble to put it mildly. So remember, we're in this together, right?'

'*Fuckers I have known.* I like it.'

Dirk changed the gear on his mountain bike. He'd bought it in Hollingsworth Cycles with his first full pay cheque from South Dublin County Libraries. Having turned down a place in Trinity College and then failing to get into art college (his portfolio was good but not good *enough*), he could now say, depending on who he was speaking to, that he was either a librarian who painted or an artist who worked in a library. He was, he convinced himself, *someone.* He wondered what it would feel like to be a fucker someone once knew. To be blacklisted by someone who polished his hoop earring every night and shone his shoes every morning. He'd grown to like Dave over these months. But there were moments, seconds even, when he felt like he had just lost a small part of himself. A spark gone, less of a polish evident. But in perspective it was nothing more, he pondered, than a thought in his head. They belted down Harcourt Street and locked their bikes to the rails of St Stephen's Green Park.

They made their way down Grafton Street. *Click click*. Dirk had designated the wooden soles with traditional nails as his unique calling card. Handmade, they were, Italian leather. *Click click*. They sang the sound of his success. The street was buzzing: buskers playing guitar very badly, long-legged girls laughing loudly, a group of guys the worse for wear. A woman sat on a plastic bag in the doorway of what was once Switzer's. She kept her dog tied with a length of old twine. She watched the two men pass her by.

'Fortune,' she shouted, a black hole where a tooth once was. 'You boys have good fortunes.'

Dirk looked at her, sure he could recognise her. She raised her hand as if to wave and then pointed straight at him.

'You,' she said, 'you *know*.'

Dirk held her gaze as they walked away. He was distinctly aware of the feel of the wallet in his breast pocket, fat with notes from the bank machine.

Dirk was back painting again. He'd discovered Kandinsky, spinning away from the Van Gogh swirls he'd once painted and catapulting his body into the squareness of boxes, completeness of circles. Everything was made up of abstract shapes. Just like he'd been told in school. They'd draw and the teacher had said always, always start with an oval. An oval for the body; a circle for the head. It was the hands that always got him. The hands that created that he couldn't assign a shape to. He'd divided his life in two: courting fun and the space where he lost himself between the brush and the stroke of paint. He once told Dave that he painted to stop the *boredom*. Dave asked him why didn't he just watch television or go to the pub.

'I'm boring,' he used to say, at the age of five, to his mother. 'No,' she'd reply with a laugh, 'you're bored not boring.' Now he realised that his five-year-old self was right; he was *boring*. There was something in him that depended on others for entertainment. Like that Nirvana song, he was here now, entertain him. When Dirk closed his eyes a flood appeared in vivid reds and hues of Mediterranean orange. Painting. There were times when he painted in the dark so that he wouldn't think. Thoughts that raced past him, stumbling in their incoherence, painted out of existence. The neatness of shapes, the smoothness of the palette, the edge a dry oil gave on a canvas, allowed a smile to sit with ease on his face. As his mind focused on the click of his heels he returned to the orange of his latest work that was in danger of turning brown, possibly and perhaps eventually becoming black.

He remembered suddenly that Dave had left his Walkman in his cycle basket. He momentarily stopped walking, sure it would definitely be gone. And there probably would be a few tapes as well; he always brought three or four with him. But Dave would laugh it off, in that actor-ish way of his. Their double act would get them somewhere, he could feel it, he'd say, it would work with the ladies tonight. There were times when Dirk would pretend that he was dreaming, that what he said or did wouldn't have any consequences, only memories to laugh at, moments to reminisce about. Nothing, essentially, *mattered*. They were here for fun, he reminded himself as he caught up with Dave.

Instead of guessing the colour of the next car to come around the corner, his little bets now centred on which hair colour the girls they chatted up would have. Invariably he would win. Much better odds on hair colour than car colour, he thought. With the fiery red-head, he'd bring himself back to the wooden table at Aunty Sheila's, a glass of red lemonade set before him. An espresso coffee, like tar with its strength, for the girl with blue-black hair. Each night would be punctuated with bets and flashes of dream sequences as the people he met seemed to fly through his fingers like rain, never sticking, never staying, leaving him wondering. Like the oil colours in his paintings; tangible but, in another light, not quite solid enough to be there.

'That's what life is, Dirk, my man,' Dave would say. 'Fun. Party. And if you think otherwise, you're missing the point. All these people who take life too seriously, they're not living, they're just getting by. And I, for one, don't want to get by. I want to get high on life. Yes, sir,' he'd say, 'high on life itself.'

And no matter how many times Dirk heard him say this, he'd laugh. It was like the ripple effect. Dave passed things to him and he passed them around, like doling out sweets. People always ran, jumping, grabbing at the chance for an extra bit of happiness. Truth never came into it.

'You and your go-go girls,' said Dirk, shaking his head. 'What about decent conversation?'

'We all know it's the go-go girls, the girls who are – '

'willing and able – '

' – to provide us with our fun.' Dave stopped walking and stroked his chin. 'You know, now that Teresa's finally fucked off on me, I'm really in the mood.'

'Oh.' Dirk looked at him.

'What?'

'I hadn't realised she'd left you.'

'Stupid bitch. I'm well rid of her, me. Well rid of.'

'When?'

'A few months ago. There was a note on the table. I thought I mentioned it.'

Dirk watched for the same look he'd seen in Dave's face the first night they'd spoken in Vaughan's. There was nothing to be read, though. He swallowed. 'No. No you didn't *mention* that you'd split up. Anyway, how many years had you been together?'

'Man, who the fuck cares? Why would I let the fact that a woman who announces that I, as a man, am a *penis with lungs*, upset the apple cart? I'm well rid of her. And you know what?' Dave puffed his chest out, stretched his arms, his black shirt lifting to reveal a slight pot belly. 'You know what? I don't give a *fuck*. Not a flying fucking duck.' He swung his arms dramatically down again. 'So, are we off, then, Dirk, or are we off then, Dirk?'

'We're off.' Dirk smiled, deciding that it was pointless him worrying about Dave's ex-girlfriend.

'We're off to see the Wizard the wonderful Wizard of Oz, to meet some go-go girls,' sang Dave as he skipped, laughing.

Dirk walked slowly behind him. He should think about the night. The night ahead. So. The Foggy Dew. Beautiful people. People with stories. They'd meet a blonde first and then a redhead. Or maybe it would be the other way around, depending on where they went. No, it would be a strawberry blonde first and he'd drink whiskey to match her hair.

'Come *on*, a bit of life, please. We are walking models,' Dave said. 'You, my man, are the one who gets us places and I am the one who gets the girls. And I'll present you as Mister Dirk Horn, Artist and Philosopher.' Dave winked, his sandy hair in a high quiff making him look like a teddy boy in the wrong clothes.

'And that's Dirk with a D and Horn without an e. Lovely to meet you,' Dirk replied in his practised West-Brit accent. And he'd give his customary slight bow – as if he had begun a full one and forgotten to finish it – and smiling, toss his long curly black hair off his face.

*

The first victim was a peroxide blonde, in a red cat suit with flaming red lipstick. She looked like a fire, Dirk thought. A red-hot fire. He knew he'd win his little bet. Things were good.

'So, what film set did you step out of?' she said to Dave, rolling her eyes to heaven, looking at Dave's peacock blue silk shirt bellowing out under the fan. 'Pride and fucking Prejudice?'

'Could be,' Dave said, shrugging his shoulders, 'given that I'm an actor.'

'He's going to be a big star, is our Dave – aren't you?'

'Abso-fantastically-lutely. Bet your bottom dollar on me, you could.' Dave laughed. 'Dave Jones, at your service, ladies. I'll just pop to the bar for our refreshments.'

'Right. Come on Louise. We're, like, out of here.'

Dirk fiddled with the gold sovereign ring on his right finger and licked his lips.

'Married are you?' she said, suddenly interested. Her companion wiggled away.

Dirk laughed loudly, taking a swig of his Guinness, realising that he'd have to change to whiskey if he were to match her hair. 'Not on this hand. It's the wrong hand, you *silly billy.*'

Her body language relaxed. 'Sorry,' she said, suddenly embarrassed. 'That's really none of my business. I shouldn't have asked. The name's Alison, by the way.'

'I thought you said you were, like, out of here,' he said, raising his eyebrows.

'Louise is just gone to the loo. We'll be going when she's back. I mean, I wouldn't go for a married man, I'm not like that. So don't get me wrong.'

'Well, Alison, I've no intention of ever getting either married or getting involved with anyone who is or might be or was married. So, no, I have no idea what you mean.'

She started rummaging in her handbag, also red. Dirk thought it was slightly too large for a night out. It could have anything in it – a gun, an umbrella, an extra-large make-up bag filled with condoms in the hope of publicised success, Christian Dior killer red lipstick and sparkling silver mascara, the height of sophistication.

'So when you're out of here where are you going?' She was really quite pretty. Although Louise's hair appealed more, it was one of those undecided colours, not red, not brown, not dirty blonde. Somewhere in between the lot. And yet there was a strange, solid beauty in its colourless state. He decided, yes, he liked her. Sort of. He liked Louise's hair and Alison herself. If you could mould them together, then he'd be happy, he thought.

'Wherever,' she said, smiling back. 'We'll just go where the mood takes us.' She started rummaging in her bag again.

Her cheeks were either incredibly flushed or she had far too much blusher on, he thought, getting quite curious as to the contents of her large bag. He couldn't decide if it was fake or leather. He wanted to grab it and smell it; if he did that, he thought, he would know everything there was to know about her.

He leaned forward, his eyes peeled, trying to peer into the bag. 'Want to come to a party? Rathgar Road?'

'Depends.'

'A private party with film stars and artists.' He finished the pint and smacked his lips, feeling there was something monotonous about this, something the same about them all. They would cod themselves into believing his lies because they wanted to. It was the chance of excitement, the promise of difference that appealed; he knew because it was the same thing that had attracted him and kept him with Dave, going out Friday night after Friday night. Dirk had yet to find a way to capture the feeling of those nights. Nobody stayed around long enough to be worshipped or even to be loved. These were mere snatches, like snapshots or adverts, of colour, of sound. Of moments. Moments of fun. Enhanced by the Technicolor of a hair dye or the latest fashion accessory.

'Depends,' Alison said again.

Dirk liked the way she looked towards the Ladies, not bothering to hide her anxiety. He casually rested his arm on her shoulder. He smiled, flicking a curl back from his face, thinking what memory he would keep of her. A sigh? The way she watched him quietly? The way she was both attracted to and repulsed by him? The way a wrinkle appeared in her neck when she looked away from him?

'Well, I suppose it might be fun,' she said, visibly relaxing.

'You know all these people who take life too seriously, they're just getting by. And I, for one, don't want to get by in life; I want to get high on life.'

'That's a good attitude to have, I suppose. People do take things too seriously sometimes.' She bit the side of her thumbnail, fiddled with the clasp of her bag.

'High on life,' Dirk said. He stood back again. 'Finished playing with your bag, then?' She was like a baby with its pacifier. Always turning to. Always feeling for.

She reddened. 'I was just trying to check my purse for small change.' She brushed her hair back from her face.

'Getting the bus home?'

'No, I mean yes.'

Dirk suddenly felt sorry for her. He stood still with the realisation that he did not know how he should be, how he should feel. And then it occurred to him that by being a crap liar, she was making herself all the more interesting. It was this, this spark of interest that would make him happy. And really, he ran his fingers across his lips, everything, literally everything, had to do with perspective. He could see Louise walking slowly towards them. Louise's hair was definitely better, more layers, more texture. He looked across to the bar and saw Dave standing between two exceptionally attentive blondes. Dave was always the one to get the lookers; he had such a sleek manner about him. Dirk stared into his empty pint glass.

Louise looked at him. 'So, what's the party, then?'

'My companion over there will be leading the way.' He could hear his voice, clipped.

'Are those tarts coming as well?'

He closed his eyes momentarily. Maybe he should go home. The lights were too bright. He decided he disliked the handbag. In fact, he disliked both of these girls.

'Well? Are they?'

'Louise.' Dirk wagged his finger at her. 'Louise, those girls are good friends of Dave and they are most certainly not tarts as you refer to them. They are just a little short on long clothes this weather.'

'You can say that again.' Louise gave a loud snort.

'Come on,' Dirk said, 'let's join Dave and the girls. There'll be no bitchy talk. It's my party and I shall cry if I want to. Of course you're probably too young to remember that song.' He took a deep breath. A flash of the colour of whiskey changing when the ice hit it crossed his mind. He had to capture *that*. But he drank his neat. The way it was meant to be.

As he approached, he realised what Dave had. Exactly what he, Dirk, didn't have. Dave could make people really laugh. A laugh of the soul, by just being fucking Dave. He knew how to be, he could be anything and everything. He was waving a little black book in the air. So he was giving them the *fuckers I have known* routine. Or did he say the book was full of *bitches* if he was talking to girls? Dirk pushed his way up to the bar and ordered the drinks. It was time for the whiskey to get a bit of feeling into that body of his.

Dave nodded. 'So, I was saying, the party's on the Rathgar Road. A huge place, we did some filming together. You're coming, aren't you, girls?'

Dirk smiled, an arm snaking around Alison. 'Drinks, anyone?'

Alison moved away slightly and nudged Louise. 'Oh you've

been in a film. What film?'

'Yeah, I bet it's with Patrick Swayze,' Louise cooed.

They turned to face Dave.

'We're just going to powder our noses,' the blondes said in unison.

'We'll see you downstairs, then,' Dave said, 'just outside the door.'

'So,' Louise asked, 'were you with Patrick Swayze?'

'Not as glamorous as that, I'm afraid, but we have to start somewhere. Actually it's a TV advert. A major brand of washing powder.'

They snickered.

'He plays the dirty father,' Dirk said, deadpan.

Dave shook his head. 'To be truthful, both Dirk and I have worked with people like Morrissey, Def Leopard, you know, music videos and stuff. And they were looking for a model for this ad so I just, like, totally fitted the part. Isn't that right, Dirk?'

'Sure is.'

'Well, you guys have just met your number one fans,' said Louise. She snapped her bag shut.

Dirk thought then, that the silver clasp on the bag was what he'd remember.

'I just love *Dirty Dancing*,' Louise said, looking at Dirk.

*

An hour later, Dirk beckoned a group towards Stephen's Green. They followed him up Grafton Street, Louise and Alison breaking into a jig.

'Call the dancers,' shouted Dave.

Dirk, captain and pied piper for a moment, paused, held his hand in the air, calling for silence before he bowed. 'One Mister Dirk Horn at your service.'

Everyone clapped.

'To the party.' Dirk waved them onward, glad he wasn't going back for the bikes, glad that by the next day his realisation that Dave had left his beloved Walkman and tapes in the basket

69

would be obliterated, glad that for now, he was relieved of all responsibility.

Dave wolf-whistled loudly. 'Did you know that I'm so dead famous I'm actually in disguise? Right now?'

'All lies, every word out of this man's mouth is a lie. Never believe a word,' responded Dirk. 'He's just a fucking chancer.'

'And Dirk Horn should know. With a name like he's going to have a whole black book devoted to him.'

Dave laughed and the go-go girls giggled back, swapping lipstick and blusher as they pushed their freezing legs forward in their impossibly high heels towards the party.

Dirk stopped walking and breathed in the chill as the air slapped his face. He was storing the sensation as air hit his nostrils. He looked up and examined the sky. It was the colour, he concluded, that he wanted to worship.

It was the colour of boredom.

Cakes On The Piano

Death and marriage ensured Sheila McNamara was the sole remaining occupant of 57 Limekiln Drive with its glossy grass-green door. Every year it was painted by Andy Jones in his old denim dungarees.

Mary was convinced there was something more than an occasional business relationship between them. She'd arrive with flowers in an old basket made by their mammy years ago when she was in the Irish Countrywomen's Association. The sound of Dickie Rock from the open windows gave a newness to the air.

'So,' Mary would say, grinning, enjoying waiting for movement between them.

'Mary.' And Andy would nod as he wobbled on the old wooden ladder, splashes of green across his dungarees.

There were days he looked so frail he could topple over in a light wind. Supposedly, though, like Sheila, he was in his sixties.

'Ma'll get rid of it,' he'd say whenever Sheila expressed concern over the paint stains. 'She soaks them for days.'

Sheila, though glad he was cared for, was acutely aware of loneliness spreading through her like a chill. There were none of Mammy's sweaty bed sheets to be washed anymore and not even her own panties needed to be soaked to remove menstrual blood.

Nothing but plates sticky with chocolate cake needing a soak.

*

Andy liked cakes. The first time he painted the door she'd been baking. She'd made apple tart using Mammy's recipe, humming as she flaked butter and flour to make the pastry, singing as she rolled it out.

'Something smells good.'

71

'It's nothing,' she said, delighted he'd noticed, 'but sure there's too much for me, won't you have a wee slice?'

'I brought lunch,' he said, indicating a blue plastic container and avoiding her gaze.

But he did have a slice. Two, in fact, both with generous dollops of cream. They sat beside each other at the old oak kitchen table, eating their tart with small pastry forks in silence. It was all washed down with hot tea brewed in an old tannin-stained teapot.

'That hit the spot,' said Andy when he finished. 'Thanks very much Mrs MacNamara.'

'Oh,' she blushed, 'please, none of this missus business. I'm just Sheila.'

*

He was back to put the top coat on.

Sheila, relieved that Mary had stopped calling so often, made scones. Two types: cherry and plain. He tried each of them.

'The grub's so good here,' he declared rubbing his belly. 'What do I want with Ma's plain sandwiches when I can feast on your scones?'

Sheila smiled. And then they talked about showbands; the social life they no longer had. The Capitol Showband was one they both favoured but Sheila was disappointed to discover they'd attended different ballrooms. Somewhat reluctantly, she'd followed her sister Mary to the Gresham Hotel in Dublin's O'Connell Street while Andy had followed his brother Jim to the Gymnasium in Baldonnell, County Dublin.

Now Andy came a long way to where Sheila was in Terenure just to paint a door.

But still, here they were, together at her kitchen table yet again, wiping flour from their chins.

She packed a bag of scones. He hesitated, just enough to be polite, before accepting them.

'You're too good.'

'At least they'll be eaten.'

'If you ever need anything doing, you know, or ever… ' He

stopped, red-faced. 'Otherwise, next year. Or maybe before, with the heavy rain and wind those doors'll be needing regular painting… '

She laughed, uncomfortable at his embarrassment.

*

Five years later Sheila found herself busy about the house. First dusting, then moving from room to room with the carpet sweeper on its last legs and, finally, baking. Dirk was calling. In his early teenage years he'd never seemed bothered about her but now he'd call round once a week with armfuls of books from the library where he worked. She thought of him as *good*, not unlike herself as a young girl: polite and often described as *pleasant*. Her mind sometimes boggled: she was genuinely able to enjoy his company even though he wasn't her son.

She couldn't decide what his preference would be so she made a plain Madeira, apple tart and trifle. The last, though not strictly baking, was for nostalgia. It was sure to bring him back to the days when she'd have the whole family over for dinner – playing the role Mammy would have played had she been alive – and she'd make a cherry trifle with raspberry jelly and watch with pleasure as he licked the custard and cream from his lips.

The telephone sounded. As she went to pick up the receiver, she could see Dirk, his eyes a sharp blue against his dark curls.

'Aunty Sheila,' his voice sounded anxious.

'Yes, Dirk,' she said, feeling herself flush.

'How are you?'

'I'm fine. Expecting you.'

She knew *something* had come up.

'I'm so sorry,' he started. 'I just can't leave work early today.'

'I'm grand,' she heard herself saying. 'Go on, you'll be by again. I'll even make some cakes.'

'That would be great.'

She nodded to herself.

'Sorry again.'

'Don't leave it too long, now.'

He laughed. 'I won't.'

She'd put the landing light on. She'd thought briefly of placing candles around the place. They were the latest accessory, Maureen told her when she picked up her *Ireland's Own* the other day in Caffrey's. Maureen was Mrs Caffrey's daughter; it was expected that she would inherit the shop. Sheila felt strong resisting her persuasive offer of two vanilla candles for seven pounds twenty-five. Instead she bought place mats.

Sheila went down the four steps into the kitchen. Originally this had been the scullery but not even in Mammy's lifetime was it used as such. She thought the steps added a sense of passage between the drawing room, the dining room, and the kitchen. They'd always eaten in the kitchen, except for Christmas when they'd eat in the dining room, people tripping over one another as they went up the steps with bowls of jelly, rounds of sandwiches at tea and down again with plates of crumbs.

She'd laid the desserts out on the kitchen table in a tempting row. She sighed. She decided to put the kettle on anyway. She would just have to do some tasting herself. She hoped the kettle would boil quickly.

She ran a finger across the cream of one of the cakes, a trail of loneliness through its perfection. As she was pouring the boiling water into the large teapot, it seemed to sail through the air. She cried out as it smashed on the tiled floor, the skin on her shin hot and raw. 'Jesus, let's get that leg seen to,' she imagined Dirk would say, his voice sounding just like his dead father's.

*

That night as she lay in her bed with its lavender sheets, Sheila thanked God that her leg wasn't burned, that all it got was a little splash. Sheila prayed that the next guests would enjoy eating her cakes as much as she had making them. She closed her eyes, listening to the rain beating on the window, and dreamt of walking in a wheat field as a girl holding her mammy's hand.

Moments flew like the dust Sheila lifted off the piano. Months passed.

Andy didn't call at Easter, like he usually did, for hot cross buns. The number she had for him rang out. Her own telephone hadn't been tinkling lately so there was a strong possibility there was something wrong with the line. Maureen told her that there were some upgrades to the wires and that they were mistakenly cutting people off. But imagine, now you could plug a little white thing into the telephone switch that connected you with people on the other side of the world! You could write messages on your computer and the plug thing, Maureen explained, would transport the note instantly. It didn't look much but certainly it would be the end of the letter, Sheila said, shaking her head in despair. Technology, they call it, Maureen said. Plain Darwinism, Sheila mumbled as she tied her peach headscarf in a sharp knot under her chin. She left the shop with the *Divine Word* under her arm. It was evident that Maureen, for all her chat, was of another generation.

*

It was nearing summer and, in hopeful preparation for Andy's painting, Sheila decided to try out new cakes. By four o'clock she was exhausted. She plumped up her pink cushion and sat on the high-backed chair in the drawing room that looked out the window. Dirk was due at half past.

She smiled, relieved: she'd filled the kitchen table with cakes and she'd made so many variations of Victoria sponges that they'd streamed, almost like children, onto the piano. The shimmer of white icing sugar delighted her as the sun shone through the thin but elaborately decorated net curtain. Her nose twitched at the smell of freshly baked cakes. Mammy and Daddy's wedding plates were set on the table; china with patterns of tiny roses round the edges. A slice of plain Victoria sponge looking just delightful.

Dirk's shadow approached the door. Before he'd pressed the

bell or touched the brass knocker, Sheila was there. Before he'd a chance to ask how she was, Sheila was telling him about her baking spree.

'Now I know,' she was saying, 'I said I was going to take it easy but you see, with Andy... ' She could not prevent herself from blushing. 'He'll be coming, you know, as usual, to paint the door, so I said I'd try out a few cakes so you can tell me which is the best... '

'Sheila, I'd be honoured.' Dirk stopped in the hallway. 'Are those... cakes?'

'Oh!' Sheila giggled. 'There wasn't enough room on the table so be a dear, Dirk, and take them down from the piano. We can sample a sliver of each.'

She felt thrilled. The shuffle and bustle of movement through the house was leading right to the exclamations of delight that would ring in her ears as the cakes were sampled.

'I must say,' Dirk said, 'the idea of cakes decorating the piano is very modern, Sheila, in fact it looks just beautiful. Aesthetically pleasing, even.'

'But what's more pleasing,' Sheila said, standing up from the kitchen chair, 'is what makes them. Come,' she said, a conspiratorial look on her face, 'come look in the gloryhole.'

Dirk ducked behind her into the little room under the stairs. There was a wire letter rack stuffed with letters, several bottles of lavender furniture polish and five shelves held up by rusty nails.

'Daddy used to keep tools, hammers, twine, bits and pieces here but now I keep my *own* odds and ends.'

In neat lines Sheila had:

Thirteen tiny bottles of essence of vanilla;
Four tins of crème caramel;
Seven boxes of icing sugar;
About twenty eggs sitting in egg-cups in a row;
Six tubs of baking powder;
Seventeen packets of caster sugar;
Three tins of golden syrup;
Four tubs of bicarbonate of soda;

76

Hanging on hooks: over-ripe bananas;
In a neat line: kiwis;
In a pristine white bowl: lemons and limes.

'Well? Isn't it *glorious*?'

Dirk picked up the crème caramel; it was two years out of date. 'What do you make with this?'

'I used to make banoffi pie, it was all the rage a few years ago.'

'Don't you keep your eggs in the fridge?'

'Oh dear boy! Didn't Mary ever tell you that eggs *simply must* be at room temperature?'

She took Dirk's arm, led him back to the kitchen, shaking her head.

'I'll tell you,' said Dirk, 'we won't be eating for a week after this.'

Sheila drummed her fingers on the table, her eyes darting from cake to cake. 'I think,' she said, cake slice in hand, 'we'll start with the plain sponge and then go for the lemon drizzle cake followed by the kiwi sponge. Kiwis just have that touch of the exotic, don't you think?'

The kiwi sponge won the day, closely followed by the lemon drizzle cake. The key lime pie – even though made with ordinary limes – was a step too far. They concluded, though, that Andy would like apple tart as much as any of the fancy cakes.

*

Sheila had her plan. She would wear her best dress, paint her lips ruby red. It was a leap year and, although the day had long passed in February on which women were traditionally permitted to propose marriage to their loved ones, she would propose to Andy on 5th July, the day he had first come to the house five years ago.

She'd telephoned and finally managed to get to an answering machine on which a woman's voice – it was hard to determine her age but Sheila supposed it was his mother – said simply 'leave a message, please'. She'd hesitated but then left a message: 'Andy, this is Sheila from 57. I need my door a fresher shade of green. I've been baking. See you on July 5th.'

The night of 4th July, Sheila could hardly sleep. She'd watched the trickle of light coming through the single glazed window with a light breeze as dawn broke, then prepared herself a hot chocolate followed by a long bath. She'd finally dressed and walked slowly up the village to Mass, stopping at Caffrey's on the way home for a chat.

But Maureen wasn't in that day.

'She's not the best,' said Mrs Caffrey. 'There's a baby on the way,' she leaned forward, whispering.

Sheila left with *Ireland's Own,* her spirits faltering. Perhaps this wasn't a good idea; it was a year since she'd seen him, after all. But still.

*

The baking was done: cakes on the piano; tarts on the table.

Everything was set. She gave the house another quick clean and took some time to rearrange her hair. She ate her portion of the ham sandwiches she'd made for their lunch.

That afternoon Mary arrived, Mammy's basket filled with coral gladioli. Two small treats were wrapped in tissue paper.

'What's this in aid of?' Mary nodded at the dress, cinched in at the waist, the lipstick, the heels.

'I'm tired of being nothing.'

Mary reddened.

'What's the face on you for?' Sheila asked as she cut into a fresh cream cake and dished it onto Mary's plate.

'Nothing. I just brought us two Mary cakes from Bewley's. You used to love them.'

Sheila looked at the cream cake and frowned.

'But I can have them with Dirk, later…' She paused, biting her lip.

Sheila shrugged; her shoulders stiff.

Mary sighed. 'I'm worried… about Dirk.'

'You should leave him be. He's a good lad.'

Mary shrugged. She took a forkful of cake. 'This is one of the best you've made. I don't know why you don't talk to Maureen and see if she'll sell a few for you.'

Sheila sighed. 'I've said this before. I will *not* take money for them. My cakes are simply for sharing. For enjoying.'

'You're not getting any younger. Why you don't want to enjoy a few extra pennies while you're still in one piece is beyond me. I mean we're just seven years away from a new century.' Mary's tone was sharp.

Sheila turned, looked out the window. It was past four o'clock. It was too late for any painting to be done now.

*

Sheila finally managed to talk to the woman whose voice she'd heard on the answering message.

The woman was sorry, she said, she'd only moved into the house three months ago. She knew nothing of the previous occupants apart from the fact that one had died from a stroke and the other had fallen from a ladder. Now that she thought of it, it was probably the man, she supposed, who'd fallen from the ladder. She wasn't sure when.

'Did you know them well?' she asked.

'No,' Sheila said, her voice a whisper, 'not well at all.'

*

Sheila put freshly made cakes, the steam rising off them, on the doorstep for passers-by to sample. She refused to try them herself. The baker, she said, could never be the taster.

Something had to be done. Dirk took some of the cakes for the readers in the local library. Mary persuaded Maureen in Caffrey's to sell the cakes for 50p each. They flew off the shelves.

Then Maureen visited number 57 with a baby girl.

'I've called her Sheila,' she said, smiling, 'after the most gentle woman I know.'

'I don't know anyone called Sheila,' Sheila said.

79

The baby let out a cry.

'I'm using my supplies,' Sheila continued. 'When they're gone, they're gone.'

Maureen looked at Mary.

'When those shelves are empty, they're empty,' Sheila concluded.

'Here's *Ireland's Own*,' Maureen said, holding it out, tears in her eyes. 'We have to be going now.'

Mary accompanied Maureen and the baby in silence to the door, where Maureen told her she was unnerved by the way Sheila's body was fading as her voice was growing stronger.

*

Sheila MacNamara stood, every morning, in a polka dot dress in front of the door with layers of glossy grass-green paint flaking away.

Around feet clad in navy patent heels sat Victoria sponges of strawberry, kiwi, jam – icing sugar sparkling in the morning light.

A voice carried above the rush hour traffic, gathering strength.

'Cakes are for sharing. Cakes are to be enjoyed.'

China Doll

The door opens to the sound of Pink Floyd. The place is packed, the smoke swirling like fog, the buzz of conversation flying through the air. *No, you can't beat the real thing here in good old Dublin town.* With every dark cloud there's a silver lining. I used to laugh at my gran for saying that but you know what? Walking into this large Georgian house at nearly midnight on a May night I feel possibility. I can almost touch the silver. Gran was right.

My fingers curl around the plastic bottle filled with vodka and Ribena in my grey parka pocket. I take a deep breath: if I am to survive this party I must *unbecome* myself.

'A girl like you... ' the bloke on the door says with a stupid cheesy grin. He steps back to let me in. 'A girl like you won't be alone for long. Come on in.'

I walk in.

'Yeah, yeah,' I reply, flicking my fingers, waving him away.

I'm used to being looked at. I was *the* girl at school, the girl who bagged Johnston after he pinched my bottom at a youth club disco. We suited each other. That is to say, we looked well together, like a matching cup and saucer: he was tall and broad shouldered and I was pretty fashionable. We were the Irish equivalent of the prom king and queen; we were the ones who knew who we'd go to the Debs with: Johnston and Angela, all in one breath.

He left me for a nurse with big boobs and curly red hair. Six weeks and three days ago. Last week I put a red streak in my blonde hair which hangs over my face. I've painted myself to look like a china doll. The lipstick is a shade too dark, like blood. In a way it suits my mood. It took me a good while to get ready, what with shaving my legs, waxing, plucking the eyebrows. All – like so many things we do – for the *just in case*. It's not that I've had many one-night stands. I've never had one, but, you know, I keep thinking that maybe I will.

'Scrumpy?' asks a guy all in black, hair down his back in a long ponytail.

'Sure.' I take the can. 'Angela.' I extend my hand, noticing a chip on the index finger nail. I've painted my nails *vixen red* to cheer myself up.

'James,' he replies.

'Hi,' I say, suddenly conscious of the effort I've made: the nails, the make-up, the tan. Yes, I've even put fake tan on, for old time's sake, like I used to wear at school. A sort of orange glow that's marginally better than red goose bumps on snow-white skin.

'You one of Dave's?'

'Who's Dave?'

'One of the hosts.' James smirks. I can tell he's glad I'm a gatecrasher. Maybe he's one too.

'Of course,' I lie.

'Like me, of course,' he echoes.

He's sort of cute in a girlish way. Ma brought me shopping after the Johnston split and bought the outfit I'm wearing: silver sparkling leggings and a black velvet top that goes on past my bum.

'That's perfect on you,' Ma said, glad, I think, that I'd finally stopped crying. 'It hits the right spots. You don't want to be too revealing. Boys don't like that. The top is just the right length.'

I resisted the urge to grind my teeth. Ma's a good mother; she only wants for my happiness.

'It'll happen,' she said to my tears, 'it'll happen again. Happiness always does.'

She was disappointed, I think, when I switched from law to architecture after a year at UCD. I just couldn't do something I didn't believe in. With the Birmingham Six and all that going on, even though they'd finally got justice in March, really, how could I sit and read those case studies pretending there was justice?

'Well, make yourself at home, Angela,' James says. He brings me back with his beam.

'Thanks.' I think then that there is little possibility of finding someone better looking or more charming than James here. But I'll still investigate. 'I'll be back in a tic.'

'Sure,' James says, his voice flat.

I wander into the room where the music is coming from.

'Hey there, pretty lady.'

I stop, cock my head to one side and smile.

'I'm Mike, a friend of Dave's. Been back in London for a bit so it's good to catch up on the Irish talent.'

Mike is six foot something, beyond pepper being wholly salt makes him all the more alluring. He was obviously once dark but is still extremely handsome. It's hard to tell his age; he's one of those people who could be fifty or sixty or even forty.

'Angela. Nice to meet you, Mike,' I say, opening my can and taking a long drink. 'So is London where you're from? Originally, like?'

'Yeah, I'm a London boy, me. Welcome to the party. Any friend of Dave's is a friend of mine.'

'Thanks,' I say, deciding that I am a friend of Dave's, wherever the hell he is. 'Great party so far.'

'Fantastic! It's not every day you sell a big name artist.'

'You're an art dealer?'

'So not just a pretty face, then?'

He's leaning against the doorway of the room where people were scrambling to form a space to dance. Something about him reminds me annoyingly of Johnston. David Bowie comes on, crackling from a scratched record. A group of girls with heavy black eyeliner sing at each other about putting on their red shoes.

'Oh that's my *song*,' says Mike as he heads for a spot on the floor.

He starts gyrating wildly, swinging a bottle round his head like a lasso. Everyone, including me, laughs. He's actually funny, I think. I take off my parka and hold it across my arm. I feel too hot, too clothed but at least I don't look like those girls racing around pretending to be a bloody train. One of them is

83

shouting, 'Choo choo train, Alison and Louise, the choo choo train.'

I finish the cider and remember the bottle in my pocket. I have a fear I might end up like those girls if I drink too much. I also have a desire to be just like them. Not a care. Not a need to care. I've told Ma I'm staying in a friend's house. She knows I won't be home. I stroke the bottle like it's my friend.

'Where's the loo?' I turn to a girl beside me.

'Down the hall,' she points, 'and just in through the kitchen. Hope you've got your own paper.'

'Shit,' I say.

She smiles. 'Here.' She hands me some tissues. 'I always come prepared.'

'Thanks.'

'No worries.'

I go down the hall which is now full of people smoking.

'Want one?'

James is offering me a spliff. I've always stayed away. Johnston never approved of anything like that. He said it would affect his performance. He now plays for the college football team. He's doing quite well, to be fair.

'Back in a minute,' I say and hurry to the loo.

There are trays of what looks like some sort of raspberry pudding on the table. A couple are seated eating the face off each other. Beside them is a girl who is crying while she stuffs her face with some of the pudding.

'Mike?' she asks as I pause to look.

I shrug my shoulders, wondering if Mike did this to her. The sink is piled high with trays, rings of remaining pudding around them. There's a large bunch of dirty plates, all colours, sitting on the draining board. Pity I missed the dinner, I think. The crying girl blows her nose loudly. Her face is streaked black with mascara and I think: that was me a few weeks ago. That was me, every day.

The girl wasn't wrong about the loo. Not only is there no toilet paper but it doesn't flush. I open my bottle and, taking a deep breath, drink, shudder and drink some more. I screw on the lid again and pee standing up. You wouldn't know what you'd catch from a loo-seat like that. My head spins. Aha. Not quite, but nearing. I've nearly *unbecome* myself, I think. I laugh loudly.

What the hell was I thinking of in Johnston? Why didn't I go for someone else? Why didn't I dump him when we left school? I think back to my class in school. There were a few nice guys. But the trouble, then, was that they all looked about *three*. I always liked a guy to look like... a guy. No mammy's boy stuff for me. The trouble...

I take another drink and flush the chain, which, of course, doesn't flush. The water sort of bubbles up and everything moves as if to overflow.

'Fuck,' I shout.

Then it gets sucked back down and then very slowly warbles its way up again, thankfully without overflowing.

'You okay in there?'

'Yeah, sorry.' I come out to find the girl with the running mascara waiting, except she's obviously seen herself in the mirror and cleaned herself up a bit. 'The loo's fucked.'

'It's been like that since I came,' she says.

'How long have you been here?'

She shrugs. 'Since eight? Nine?'

'Oh.'

She wipes her eyes. 'Mike cooked. He's a great cook. But he's a bastard so don't believe a word from his lips.'

'Thanks for the warning.' I'm acutely aware of the mix of cider, vodka and Ribena sloshing around inside me.

'Don't get me wrong,' she smiles, suddenly. 'He's not really a bad guy.'

'Sure,' I say as I finger my red streak.

'You should hang out with him, he likes you,' she says, eyebrows raised. 'I noticed that when you came in.'

'I'm not really interested.'

She shrugs. 'So are you Mike's friend?'

'Dave's, actually.'

'Yeah, Mike mentioned him. Dave, the actor, right? I must look out for him. I'm Ita by the way.'

'Angela. Listen, I'll see you later,' I say, suddenly irritated.

85

'I'll look out for you, Angela,' she shouts after me.

I'm already walking away, wondering if Johnston just saw that girl he left me for, by accident, at a party, at a bar, in the canteen, and decide to drop me?

James is still in the hallway and with a wink passes me a cigarette box and a lighter. I grin, take the joint from the box and inhale deeply. Bowie's on yet again.

'I love to dance,' I say, imagining I am in a dream. I sway out of rhythm.

'You are such a sexy dancer,' shouts Mike in my ear and drags me away from James.

I half-laugh, half-cough and tumble my way into the centre of the dancing room. I look behind. I've lost Mike to a crowd of blondes. Fuck it. I stay, dancing alone for a while, arms in the air, enjoying myself. Bastard, I think about Johnston again, that's all he was. I laugh. I fall into a corner, landing right on top of a beanbag. I laugh again and cannot stop. I finish the joint and drink from the bottle in my pocket.

Gloria Gaynor comes on and the room is invaded by hordes of girls in spectacular heels. I lie there, thinking I should be up with them screaming that I'll survive. Instead, I take another joint from the box and light it. I look around the room in the vain hope for a decent guy. I'm going to have to get up and go find Mike or James before I fall asleep, I think. I lick my lips. There's a sweet taste from them that makes me think of that strawberry dessert in the kitchen. Or was it raspberry? It was a berry dessert. Maybe there'd be some left and I could have it. I could find that girl with the mascara down her face and ask her what happened. She could tell me her story and I could tell her mine. I should put on lipstick. I hold the joint between my teeth and apply my too-dark lipstick. Gloria Gaynor fades and Depeche Mode comes on. Who's in control of the music, I wonder.

There's a guy who's been by the door for a while, I think. He's wearing all black. He's tall with curly hair. I wave at him. I can't really see for the smoke but he looks sort of cool. He might be fun to talk to. I cough again as he comes over to me. As he approaches I think there is something familiar about him.

He finishes a cigarette with a long exhalation of smoke and stands, open-mouthed, staring.

'What?' I manage.

He rubs his eyes and I feel a flutter in my stomach watching those long fingers. Piano fingers, my gran would have called them. I take another drag from my now weak-willed joint and smile as I realise that I can say anything and he won't know if I am just a big bullshitter. And I'll just walk right out of the party, hail a taxi and go home to Ma, laughing all the way. I had *fun* I'll say to her.

'How are you?' he asks and reaches out for my hand, blinking.

I wiggle in the beanbag trying to sit up straight. 'Jesus fucking Christ.'

'You only recognise me now?'

I shake my head, lying. 'No, I… yes… I'm just so fucking happy to see you.'

He shrugs his shoulders. Dirk shrugs his shoulders. Dirk from my class and there he is, standing in front of me smiling, shrugging his shoulders, looking better, far better than I ever could have remembered him.

'It is,' I say, 'it is Dirk, isn't it?'

He laughs. 'And it is Angela fucking Quinn.'

'Yip. That's me.'

'I'm a librarian,' he says, 'I mean, an artist. Just sold a painting for a pretty penny.'

'Wow.' I'm thinking he was the artist Mike was on about. 'Wow,' I say again.

He laughs. 'I work in a library but I'm really an artist.'

I nod.

'You look good.' He sighs. 'What are you up to?'

'I'm an architect. Wouldn't think so by looking at me now, though, would you?' For some reason I wag my finger at him.

He squashes himself onto the beanbag beside me. 'Now tell me, what's a girl like you doing at a dodgy art dealer's party? And where the hell is your man of the day, Johnston?'

I fiddle with my fingers, flicking them up and down. I shake my head. 'I was at a loose end, just broke up with Johnston –

don't even ask about him — an idiot, so yeah… '

'Ace.' He runs his fingers through his hair. 'Johnston changed when we finished primary school. He grew into an asshole.'

'Dirk, this is *ace*.' I look at my hands again.

'So. Besides *him,* who do we know about?' He counts the names on his fingers, looking bored. 'Cathy went to New York. In publishing, I think. Richard's in England. Somewhere up north, Durham or somewhere. And…' He trails off.

And I have an urge to just hug him. There's something still in him that was there before. Something aloof, lost, a hovering sadness I want to touch. But that could just be the spiff.

'Dirk fucking Horn.'

He grins. 'Never thought I'd hear you curse. Miss Perfect.'

'Ha, that was all a clever façade. I wasn't perfect at all.'

He leans his head against mine then turns to look at me properly. 'So what about you? Are you working? Who do you hang out with? Tell me *everything.*'

'Well, in college I met so many people, I just couldn't keep up with the two sets of friends, you know, between studying and now starting my masters. And, of course, people change and I changed and – '

He's staring at me, open-mouthed.

' – stop fucking staring at me, Dirk.'

'Angela,' he whispers.

I shake my head. 'I kept those poems you wrote for me, you know.'

'Really?'

I wonder why I never threw them away, even when I was with Johnston. They're still in the wooden box I stuffed them in the day he gave them to me. I still remember how his hands shook as he passed the envelope along the desks, my name as whispers fluttering in the air. I cried when I read the first one. It was like one of Shelley's poems. It hit me in a way that all of Johnston's flowers and kisses combined never did.

'We should get out of here,' he says, 'go get a coffee, somewhere we can talk properly.'

'I always liked you,' I say, immediately regretting it, but I keep on going. 'I was just no competition for Cathy...' As I let my voice trail off, I decide that I will kiss him. He's still staring at me as if I'm some sort of exotic fruit in the supermarket with a name nobody can pronounce.

He whispers again, 'You're still beautiful.'

I think of asking him to write me a poem, a love poem, right now. I think of telling him that I'm really a loser, that I hated myself in school and that, truth be told, I'm still not enamoured. I think of telling him that we'll never see each other after tonight so nothing matters.

He opens his arms. I hurl myself right into the space of warmth he's created, knowing that my eyeliner and mascara will leave their calling cards. I'm laughing. I'm laughing loudly as the tears roll down my face. I must look like that other girl, now, with my mascara running but nothing matters. Roxy Music comes on. My hands are dancing above my head.

I still haven't figured out how to *unbecome* myself.

But it will happen some time, again.

Through The Looking Glass

There are five uncles of your father who are alcoholics.
Alcoholism runs in genes, skipping generations.

I am boxed, trapped, hemmed in by something invisible,
without a name.

Before you realise, it's taken over you.

I tell myself a story, of fudge, turkish delight, things with
colour, taste and smell. Magnolias are beautiful except we don't
have them in this country. Lilac blooms, its heady scent
intoxicating.

You think you know what you're doing but you don't. I can see
what's happening to you. I can tell you what is going to happen.
I am fine. It skipped me. The other children are too young for
us to tell yet. Which means it has to be –

I've a note in my pocket with which I will buy vodka.
I've not told Dad that he's broken up with me.

Time is on your side.

I hate when I arrive early at parties. The awkward silences, the
nods and smiles and the tick tock of my father's old watch on
my thin wrist.
I follow the sound of clattering plates into the kitchen where a
guy is pouring thick red syrup on top of an uncooked cake
mixture. There are two large trays.
'Hey,' he says and winks at me.
'Ita,' I say. 'Sorry I'm early.'
'Mike,' he says. 'Glad you are.'

90

I laugh.

'Just getting these into the oven,' he says, 'people always like a bit of grub. You should try some when it's done. Well worth it.'

'Sure,' I say. 'What is it?'

He laughs. 'Mike's raspberry cake.'

'Sounds good.'

'Sit down, I'll be back in a sec. Just going to change.'

I sit down at the wobbly table. Maybe Mike's the one to cheer me up.

Five out of seven males is over fifty percent.

And before that there were twelve out of thirteen; three of them women.

The odds are high.

Good, even.

While I wait for the cakes to do, I drink the vodka. I've mistimed everything.

Before I know it the vodka's gone.

'Why the long face?' asks Mike who suddenly looks dashing in jeans and tux.

'You don't want to know,' I mumble.

'Oh but I do. I've always wanted to be an agony aunt. Besides, we can't eat in silence,' he adds as he plonks his bulk on a chair beside me.

You're not staying here if you come home in that state again. While you're under this roof, you're my responsibility.

Mike is handing me fistfuls of tissues. I try to blow my anger onto them.

I stuff my face with the incredibly ugly looking but amazingly tasty pudding.

Mine is on a pink plate; Mike's on a blue.

It's a rainbow house, I think, looking at the tray and dish pile in the sink growing higher and higher.

'Your mascara's run down your face,' Mike says in a

fatherly voice.
I wonder where my five uncles, three great-aunts are
now.
The mascara weeps onto the gossamer tissue.
I wiped it so roughly across my cheek that it tears.

On the count of
five,
four, three –

Two minutes pass.
I sigh.

One.

Mike's strong arms are around me, my head spinning and light.
I am contained.
There will be no breaking loose tonight.

Craic

The pizza place just off Grafton Street was less than half full, though the noise level was soon to change as the first of the birthday celebrations got underway. Dave Jones had hit the big Three-O.

'I'll have a pepperoni and a diet coke,' said Angela, smiling at the waiter. She turned to Dirk. 'What are you going for?'

'I'm not sure,' he said, turning the menu around in his hands.

'Jesus, just choose something.' Dave was unable to hide his irritation.

'You go on, Dave.' Dirk cleared his throat loudly, flicked to the front of the menu again. Starters. He read down through the list. Garlic bread, various salads, soup of the day. Fucking uninspiring. He turned to the mains. Spaghetti Bolognaise. Lasagne. Pizzas. Chicken à la king.

'Shall I give you a little more time?' suggested the waiter, pen poised.

'I'll have me old favourite, spag bol,' said Dave. 'Can't go wrong there.'

'For me the house salad to start and the, em,' began Mike, 'em, I'll go for the mighty meaty pizza with extra cheese.' He sat back and rubbed his belly.

'Very good,' replied the waiter. 'And you, sir, have you decided?'

Dirk looked at Angela, his face blank. 'I can't,' he said.

'You can't what?'

'Pick something for me, will you?'

Dave shuffled his feet under the table. 'Will you bring this fella a shot of tequila? It's his nerves, so it is. He's a pretty sour bollix when it comes to celebrating birthdays that aren't his.'

The waiter nodded and disappeared.

'I don't want tequila, Dave.'

'Yes, you do. Look at you, you miserable fuck. We're all out

93

here for me birthday and you're sitting there, like a giant fucking nervous tic. You're doing me head in, you are. Doing me head in.'

'A bottle. Why don't we get a bottle?' suggested Mike. 'It's bloody freezing in here.'

Angela shivered. 'That's what you get going to cheap restaurants.'

'If I had my way we would have gone to South Street,' said Dave. 'That'd be much better.'

'Why didn't we?' asked Dirk, looking around.

'Because you said we'd get three courses for a tenner.'

'Oh yeah.' Dirk's fists sat clenched on his knee. Ripples of nerves ran up his back, tickling his neck, hovering. He scratched his neck and hairline.

'But of course dickhead forgot that was the fucking lunchtime offer, didn't he?'

Dirk giggled. He'd started to sweat. He should get some fresh air, he thought. But if he left he might not be able to bring himself to go back in again.

'Hey does anyone remember Sides, that brilliant nightclub that used to be on, what's the name of the street?' Mike asked scratching his head.

'Is *Jose Cuervo* alright for you?' said the waiter holding the bottle as if it were wine.

Dirk looked at him. He looked bored and his hair was greasy. He probably needed a good bath. It had been Dave's suggestion to go out for a meal, to be civilised. He said it would help impress Angela; the ladies always love a good feed. Dirk and Angela were on their fourth month of official coupledom. They met two or three times every week, taking in cinemas, art galleries. At weekends they followed Dave or Mike to where the best party was on. Going out was habit now, something which had lost any nuance of originality. Dirk had asked Mike to the birthday dinner because he knew Dave wouldn't want to feel piggy in the middle with him and Angela. He chewed on the corner of his lip; Dave, Angela and Mike genuinely got on well. When he watched them interact he saw a naturalness to the conversation, in the way they moved their bodies in and out of vision. There were no arms crossed across chests, no turn of the head. They were, most of all, he concluded, relaxed.

'Dirk,' Angela nudged him. 'The man's asking you a question.'

'Of course,' he replied, flicking a curl. 'Cuervo is fine. Please, bring one for everyone.' He gestured across the table. 'You know,' he said, swinging on his chair as the waiter went off to get more shot glasses. 'This was a fucking ace idea, Dave. It's going to be a good one. I can feel it.'

'Let's get to it, then. Tequila all around. *Andale!*' Angela tied her hair into a ponytail. It was all the one colour now; she'd bleached the dyed red streak back to its natural blonde state.

'We need some lemon, please,' said Dave, grabbing the waiter's elbow as he tried to move away.

'Certainly, sir.'

'Jesus, what's with the sir?' said Mike.

'So, as the honorary lady, I'll go first.' Angela looked at Dirk and frowned.

Dirk looked away; glad he hadn't offered to pour. He turned his gaze outside and concentrated on a couple walking past. They were walking arm in arm, chatting, and paused to look in. The girl's face came up level to his and stared. Then she burst out laughing.

Dirk could hear Angela's gasp after downing the shot. He could feel her nudging him. He breathed on the window, smiling at the little circle of cloudy breath. He rubbed it out with one wipe of his little finger. Obliterated, he thought.

'Thanks,' Dave was saying to the waiter. 'He knows what he wants now, if you want to, like, take his order.'

'I'll have the same as him,' said Dirk, looking the waiter in the eye. 'That man there, the one who ordered the mighty meaty to show what a man he is.'

Angela kicked him under the table.

'And,' he continued, 'a bottle of your finest house red. Won't anyone join me?' He scanned the silent faces in front of him.

'A bottle of red never did anyone any harm and it's my birthday.' Dave spoke quietly.

'We can bring you a cake, sir, for your birthday, sir,'

suggested the waiter.

'Oh yes, please, a cake… sir.' Dave sniggered.

'Very well.' The waiter clicked across the restaurant.

'You know something?' Dave said looking at Dirk. 'I've an audition next week, for a part on *Fair City*.'

'Wow, that's great news,' said Angela leaning over the table and patting his arm. 'I'm delighted for you, Dave. Well done. It's good to hear someone's doing okay in these crap times.'

Dirk picked up his glass and poured himself a shot. He downed it and shook his head.

'Of course, he just happened to meet the man of the moment at the party the other week,' said Mike.

'Really?' Dirk looked at Dave. 'You never said anything.'

'You didn't come to that party. I was waiting to tell you tonight, you know, that we're all together. Although – '

'Go on,' said Mike, smiling, 'there's always an "although" with you, go on.'

'Although,' said Dave laughing, 'I said to the gang we'd be in *Rí Rá* later.'

'Brilliant stuff, I couldn't have thought of a better place.' Mike chuckled to himself. 'We'll have a good old dance there.'

Dirk looked out the window again. It was too dark to see any of the people passing in the distance and nobody came close to the window. He breathed on it again and rubbed it out straight away. He momentarily considered how much force it would take to break it.

'Oh, *Rí Rá*, we haven't been there in a while,' said Angela. 'When I think back to all those discos I used to go to when I was, what, fifteen? Such craic we used to have, I mean – '

'It'll be packed,' said Dirk loudly. 'It'll be hot and sweaty and packed.'

'They were good times, they were, in the eighties,' said Dave. 'Jesus, seems aeons ago.'

'Thanks,' Dirk said to the waiter, who showed him the bottle. 'That'll do.' He shook his head. 'No, I don't want to taste.'

'I'll taste,' said Dave. 'I love tasting.'

'Did I ever tell you,' said Mike, 'about the time me and the lads nicked a box of *Bazookas* from the corner shop. Owned by

96

an Indian guy, I think, a right grump.'

Angela laughed. 'Go on.'

'Well, it was a dare – '

'Doesn't everything start as dare?' asked Dirk. 'Dating, conception, dying… '

The waiter returned with the main courses and Mike's salad.

'This looks good,' Dave said, starting to eat.

'Not bad at all.'

'A dare?' Dirk repeated. He picked up a fork and lifted some pepperoni from the pizza, stared at it.

Mike rolled his eyes. 'A starter is a starter, not part of the main course.'

'What?' Dave looked at him.

'Oh forget it. Anyone for salad?'

Mike shrugged and started eating.

'A dare?' repeated Dirk.

'Yeah, anyway, in I go and grab the box. We never ran so fucking fast in our lives. Down to the green bit we called a field behind the houses.'

'Did you get caught?'

'We made sure we didn't,' said Mike with his mouth full. 'We sat there, on the wet grass and chewed every last one of them.'

Dave shook his head. 'Weren't your bleedin' jaws killing you?'

'Yeah, and the thing is, we couldn't say *anything*. We'd have been killed. But the best bit – ' He took some wine.

'Not bad, sure it isn't?' Angela raised her glass.

Dirk clinked her glass and winked. He ate several slices of pizza in quick succession.

'The best bit was that my fucking piss was pink.'

Angela and Mike laughed. Dirk looked at them. What the fuck was so funny about *that*? The cheese sat in his stomach like a pile of bullets. 'That wine is fucking acid,' he said as he finished his glass. Out of the corner of his eye he could see a waiter carrying a cake full of candles towards them. He had a broad smile on his face, ensuring the customers would smile, cock their heads and sing 'happy birthday', thinking what a wonderful restaurant it was.

'Oh, the cake,' said Angela. 'God, you don't look thirty. Sure he doesn't, Dirk? He looks much younger.'

Dirk shrugged.

'Speech, speech, speech,' cooed Mike.

'Customers,' called out the waiter, 'please join us in singing a very happy birthday to our fine friend Dave Jones here.'

Everyone in the restaurant stood up and started clapping slowly as the waiter led the singing. Dirk looked at Dave. Angela was right. He didn't look thirty at all. He looked young and vibrant. He *was* young and vibrant, even if he did look mortified at all the attention. But he loved it, so he did. Dirk mouthed the words, his head spinning. He knew he should go home but it would be good to have a bit of a dance, get some energy again, he needed to get himself out of this mood he was in. Maybe Dave would have a few pills or something.

'Hey,' he turned to Dave. 'Happy birthday, man, you old fucker.'

'Old? What I wouldn't give to be only thirty again,' said Mike as he hugged Dave.

'Happy birthday to the finest actor in all of Dublin,' said Angela as she kissed him on the cheek.

'Oh now,' said Dave, high-pitched, 'no kissing allowed, you're already taken, my lady, aren't you?'

'If I had my way – ' started Mike.

'If you had your way,' continued Dave, 'you'd have had her the night you sold Dirk's painting instead of setting them up for the night with your little cocktail of pills!'

*

'Which level a'we on?' Dirk swayed and grabbed hold of the bar.

'What do you mean which level? There is only one level, you ponce. Where are you going? The jacks?'

'Aw, don't be mean to your best friend, Dave. C'mon. We've been friends, like, it feel likes, forever, c'mon, man.'

'Dirk, you've had enough. Come on. Let's get you home and call it a night. Angela says she's tired.'

'F'ck off. I'm grand. Just need to take a piss. Anyway Angela

98

can take care o' herself. She's a big girl.' He laughed.

'Well, let's get you into the fucking jacks for Christ's sake.'

'Let-go-o-me-you-fuckhead. I'm not a kid.' Dirk pushed him away and, as he stumbled towards the toilets, he briefly turned to see Dave shake his head and walk away.

He fumbled with his zip, urinated into the urinal, outside it and onto his trousers. Out of the corner of his eye he saw Mike beside him.

'What the fuck is wrong with you? You're ruining his birthday.'

'Not.'

'You are. He was making great headway with those girls, that blonde one, till you said she looked like a horse.'

'Well, she does.'

'Yeah, but fuck off, you don't have to say it, do you?'

'Am saying what I see.'

'Look at you.'

'Look at you.'

'Don't, Dirk. Don't fuck this up.'

'Don't fuck this up. We're at a nightclub. What's there to fuck up?'

'If Dave blacklists you, you're history, mate.'

'Big fucking deal.'

'Yeah it is, actually.' Mike kicked the wall. 'You didn't have to come tonight if you didn't want to. Myself and Dave could have just gone out, he'd have been happy to leave you and Angela out of it.'

Dirk started whistling *London Bridge is Falling Down.*

'Dirk.' Mike turned a tap on, washed his hands. '*Please.* Whatever is going through that head of yours… stop this crap.'

The whistling stopped. 'I said, in case you didn't hear me, big fucking deal. Or are you deaf?'

Mike dried his hands with paper towels. 'You know, I don't take on drunks in my gallery.'

'Who says I want to be in your poxy gallery any more? Don't I have a bloody job already?'

'You serious?'

'You serious?'

Mike slapped Dirk on the back. 'Right then.'

Dirk cracked his knuckles.

'Okay, suit yourself, mate. Suit your fucking self.' Mike walked towards the door.

'I've got Angela,' Dirk shouted after him. 'Who do you have?'

Without looking back Mike gave him the finger. The door closed shut behind him.

Dirk turned to the sink and splashed water on his face. He tried and failed to focus on his reflection. He banged his fist against the mirror.

Then drew back with the realisation that he didn't have enough strength to smash it.

Brushstroke

You've slept on the floor again. Fighting with the brush. You can hear your mother knocking on the door.

'Come on, time to get up. Jesus, you're worse than a child!'

You shake your head and stand up, stretching your arms in the air, yawning.

'Yeah,' you shout back. You stare at the door, its freshly painted gloss willing you to go at it with the brush.

'You're not the only one who can take a brush in his hand,' she said a few weeks ago. 'At least my painting is useful,' she added, an edge to her voice.

You could just see her painting those doors again. You chose not to respond to that edge in her voice and instead savaged the canvas, the brushes scattered on the floor as you felt your way with the paint, just as you did when you were a boy.

It was the same feeling you got when you swam in the sea on the first day of the New Year. You'd only done it once – as a dare – but there was something magical about it. Like a reminder that you were alive.

Now you look at what you'd stayed up until after five in the morning for – a canvas painted black.

Black nail marks.

Broad, black strokes done with fist and fingers.

In art class, you were told to drop the black. And you loved writing in green pen, but in English class, they wouldn't let you. You haven't changed and as you run your fingers over the welts of black, you feel cheated. Balance does not come easy.

You cooked a fry just because you remembered the taste of the salt on your skin, just because you suddenly felt like you needed to remind her that you were alive. You weren't just there. Or some sort of thing to be put up with. You love her. Because she is your mother. But it is beyond duty, this love. It is something you try not to think about. She didn't know how to take the cooked breakfast complete with napkin. She ate it as if it was poison. Still, you could tell she was happy. It was a silent apology for your weeks of speechlessness.

*

A few months ago your best friend told you he'd rid you of it. Soon you'd be relieved of this burden of books and purgatory of painting (it was running right through you, that much you could feel) and in its place, you'd have fun. He promised to knock it out of you in no time.

Your girlfriend said it set you apart, this earnestness. She didn't have to try as hard with you – you were so accepting of who she was. You were smiling as she said it, glad of it, happy it was you she had picked. And when she kissed you on the cheek you caught the smell of her lipstick.

Suddenly you felt less male.

The best thing, you decided, was to get out. Out of the house and start afresh. You bought a new sketchpad and a set of fancy pencils. You hopped on the bus to Tallaght and walked the rest of the way. There would hardly be anyone there, you'd reasoned. But, as you started your ascent up Montpelier Hill, you spotted another man, tall, thin and alone. So you followed him. Up the mountain path.

He found some sort of herb on the banks of a tiny river. You took him in, his wholeness, his solidity.

He ate some; he bagged some.

There, before you, was Aquinas's perfection. Something useful. Something complete.

And you stood, a few feet behind, your sketchbook becoming marked with your sweat. You watched him, your mouth chewing as he ate, your legs twitching because you were still.

'Want some?' he turned and asked, a leaf dangling down his chin.

'What is it?'

'Watercress. Gorgeous in salads.' He flicked his long fringe away from his face.

So you ate some; you drew some.

'Not bad,' he conceded, eyeing the paper.

'I'm an artist,' you said.

'So it would seem.' He smiled. 'Well, nice to meet you but I've got to get going.'

When his bobbing head was out of sight you waved after him.

You continued the climb and reached the ruins of the Hell Fire Club. Even in its silence, it didn't speak. And you left, with just a sketchbook with four neat outlines of watercress, each inside a circle.

*

You'd spent most of your life avoiding labels but you'd taken this one on quite willingly.

Artist. Then, once you had said it, it was gone.

Now, every day, you keep the pencil moving across the paper as you write the stories of the pictures you will paint. You write to keep the strokes even and measured. You look at a pile of books in the corner and pull out one that you haven't read in years. You hold it up to the light. The pages are peppered with greasy fingerprints, transparent, a reminder of a connection long gone. A reminder of when there was joy. When eating chipper chips and turning the pages of a book was all you hoped for.

You look for a sign. A glint of silver catches your eye.

And you take it. And you place the lead on the canvas and turn the compass. A smile creeps onto your face as the scratch of the silver point completes a circle.

You stand back and look at its roundness, an indent on the canvas.

Perfection, you whisper.

A Chill

It's late August. You, Dirk Horn, are cementing or saving or committing to your relationship. These are words she, Angela Quinn, has used. Their meaning is beyond you, somehow.

On the train journey from the east to the west of the country. In silence you sat side by side. She flicked through a guidebook to the best pubs in the west, or north west to be a little more precise. You re-read an old faithful, as your mother would have termed it. Sartre's *Nausea*. It's a book you read as a moody teenager with your first girlfriend. She read it later in university and told you you'd got it all wrong. You're revisiting it, to be bull-headed, but also hoping for something else.

Angela has brought you to Maigh O. *The plain of the yews*. Known by the anglicised Mayo. Mayo is magic, the guidebook informs you. You sneer but still the landscape draws you in, the space, the greyness of the rock, the sparkle on the sea. It edges you towards movement. Past Grace O'Malley's castles between Mulranny and Newport, the Moy enticing you with its salmon, trout and pike. Achill Island willing you to be a different type of tourist; to stay. Maigh O. The plain of the yews. There's something about those trees that warms your insides.

The Bed and Breakfast she booked is welcoming, with views of Croagh Patrick. It's cosy, homely. There is a clatter of kids tiptoeing around, warned within an inch of their lives not to be noisy when there are guests. When you arrived they were out the back having a water fight with a hose and some water pistols, their laughter almost infectious.

'Isn't the weather just powerful?' the lady of the house said, beaming.

Angela agreed and you let her do the talking, nodding when it seemed appropriate. You heard her confirm that you'd be staying for two nights, home on the Sunday after Mass. Her voice doesn't betray the fact that like you she only goes to churches for christenings, weddings and funerals. The woman is house proud; you can see she's polished the Sacred Heart in the hall.

That evening you watched Angela brush her blonde hair – so long now it was like a child's. She sat on the chair in front of the old dressing table with a mirror full of scratches, patches of rust peeping through. The glass shining with a vinegar polish. Croagh Patrick in its silence drew your gaze into the distance to the window. She brushed her hair slowly, like she was trying to dance with you, tilting her head, static flying off the ends. She watched your face in the reflection as your gaze faltered between the beauty outside and in the room.

'I bet you're glad you're not a woman,' she said noticing you watching her.

You felt the same way you used to feel when you were a kid caught taking an extra biscuit from the jar.

'It's just so high maintenance being a woman. All the parts you have to look after.'

'Like you, my lady.' You played the part very well, letting your smile linger, while you wondered how you'd catch the stray hair on her face with your paintbrush. The way the light was catching pieces of her, laying shadows across her face, her happy, happy face.

Then she threw the brush at you. 'But I am a lady. *I am.*'

You lost yourself in the lingering warm kiss with her. She looked at you dreamily. In love.

'I can't think of words to describe you,' you said, meaning it.

'But now that you have me you don't need to describe me.'

'Angela, I want to. I want to write something, I want to paint you. But I can't.'

'Too inspiring?'

You half-thought she was right, as she licked her lips, that mock-seduction that she enjoyed so much.

'Maybe,' you said, 'I'm just not meant to paint, despite what everyone's saying.'

'Come on,' she said, gesturing towards the bed, 'let's enjoy ourselves.'

You followed her as she smiled and walked over to the

window, closing the pink and beige floral curtains on the grey of the rock on the mountains.

You undressed slowly, soundlessly, before climbing into bed.

You kissed and moved in time with her, trying to capture and keep the heat that passed between you. Not a word spoken.

You lay on your side, gazing at the small of her back, listening as she murmured, tossing and turning, knowing you'd disappointed her again.

*

'So, will we?' Angela asks, smiling, pointing towards the rocky path ahead.

Croagh Patrick stands in front, its beauty beckoning, its conical shape looming above. Clouds race across the sky hunted by wind. There's a nip in the air. You can smell the brightness on its way.

'It's definitely worth the climb,' she coaxes.

Up close it's less majestic. Up close everything feels colder. There's no window to shelter harshness. The famine memorial made of skeletons repulses you. History, you think, is in books, not real, not visible.

'So,' you ask her, turning away from the memorial, 'when was the last time you climbed up, then?'

Angela is tying her hair back in a ponytail. 'Keeps the hair off my face.'

You nod, tired of her need to explain everything.

'I've been up here countless times,' she adds.

'Impressive.' You're not surprised at all.

'We used to be dragged here as kids. *Up that hill,* my mother would say. Up that bleeding hill again! I hated it but loved it too, you know? Those rituals that you outwardly hate, they sort of make you.'

You scratch your head, looking up at the summit, trying to think of a childhood ritual. You picture your mother, as you walked down the centre aisle from the altar, having eaten your first host. You made your First Holy Communion, your first public accomplishment. Your mother had a face on her. She's

106

still a woman who is far from her name: Mary. You look at Angela, her hands on her hips.

'Well?' she doesn't hide her irritation.

'Yeah,' you say, feeling almost tearful, 'but you were a kid then. When was the last time – ?'

'Probably before I went to college.' Angela pauses. 'I'd stupidly said I'd climb Croagh Patrick if I got into college.'

'And you did.'

'I swore after that I'd never do it again. I had to dump the runners afterwards. Mind you, it didn't help that the weather was shite. What about you?'

'Never been here. Never been up it.' You wonder why neither of you talked about climbing the mountain on the train. 'Runners?' you ask. 'Why didn't you do it in your bare feet?'

'We weren't *that* religious.' She laughs. 'Dirk, I just can't believe this is the first time you've come here. It's only, like, one of the national monuments. What, didn't Sepp want to go?'

'My father?' You almost laugh. 'No. Weirdly, German and Protestant, he *did* want to climb this mountain. In fact, he came on his own a good few times. After conferences and stuff, he'd add a weekend on, a bit of quiet for himself.'

'Oh.' She looks at you from the corner of her eye.

'Mary said it was for religious freaks, all that crawling on your hands and knees, your bleeding feet. And for what? All to see a bloody bell.'

'Oh come on, it's fun as well. It's more than a bell, anyway. It's where St Patrick banished the snakes!'

'Huh,' you say, sounding like your mother. 'That's just tourist propaganda.'

'It's history, heritage. Well it's a good job your mother doesn't know I'm dragging you up here or she'd hunt me out of the house.'

'You know she adores you.'

This is true. Your mother adores your girlfriend so much, it's nauseating. Suddenly you want to climb Croagh Patrick more than anything; you want to feel the pull on your muscles, hear your breath struggle, feel that blast of wind on your face. There's yet another group of tourists, hopping, rubbing their feet, braving the sharp rocks, pilgrims for an hour.

'It's funny how they all think you have to climb it in your bare feet,' Angela laughs. 'I wouldn't like to be a chiropodist working on those feet later, would you?' She looks at your feet. 'Nor yours, for that matter. Why didn't you bring hiking boots?'

'Eh, that would be because I don't possess a pair of hiking or walking boots.' You rub your hands together. 'But I'm still going to climb up to the summit,' you say, smug at the surprise in her eyes.

'Right then, why don't we see who's got the most staying power? What about that?'

Angela jumps and bounds ahead, looking behind, laughing. 'Come on, you're like an old man. I'm so going to beat you.'

There's a nagging feeling slowing you down, clawing at your back, making it hard to breathe. You glance up when you hear her voice, drawn to her optimism and fast feet. *Come on*, you say to yourself. This is your day with your girlfriend.

'Hang on,' you call after her.

It's a tougher climb than even she'd anticipated and it takes over forty minutes just to reach St Patrick's Statue, the first stop on the traditional pilgrimage. You have a Mars bar each and a quick drink of water. Angela, as ever, has thought of everything.

'I knew you wouldn't bring any of those things, so I packed for you,' she announces, her voice so chirpy it's almost pitched high enough to be comical. 'That's why my bag was so heavy when you lifted it onto the train.'

'And here was me thinking it was shoes.'

'Oh, ha bloody ha.'

'Come on,' you say after walking around the statue, your voice breathless. It's somehow pathetic, this version of Patrick, with his staff in one hand and a shamrock in the other. Who or what would he banish from the island now?

'Let's go find a nice pub and get a good lunch,' you say, clearing your throat.

Angela frowns and shakes her head. 'Oh come on. There's no reason for you not to finish the climb other than your laziness. Let's keep at it.'

You look up at Patrick again. His beard has merged with his

vestments, his deep-set eyes almost closed, his nose Roman.

'You know Dave and I had a bet, that you wouldn't do it.' She has her hands on her hips again. She's almost ugly with annoyance.

'Lazy? Is that how you see me?' You thought you'd feel alive, somehow, the way you thought the mountain was calling you. But you feel nothing. Nothing but a chill.

'Oh, come on. You know that's not true. I'm just saying that, you know, we planned this – we said we'd do the climb. We said we'd do it *for us*.' Angela rubs your arm. 'I mean this is the first time we've been away together, you know. It's something special. Let's mark it.'

You shake your head. 'Nope.'

'You can't let Dave win a bet with me.'

You give a little laugh. Dave is your best friend who you feel nothing but hatred for, right now. Your head feels light.

She smiles; she knows. 'That's better,' she says. 'Cigarette?'

You look at her. Her face is bright, full of energy.

'Well?'

'Okay, then,' you speak slowly, your voice echoing. You look at her again and there's an intense pressure building. You can feel it and suddenly you want to scream at her. To shout that *no* you don't want to climb, you don't want to walk, even. You don't care about a stupid bet with Dave. You just want to lie. And it isn't to do with religion. It's nothing to do with your relationship – she'd start saying you weren't happy with her again – but it was just, simply, because you did not *want* to.

'I don't want a fucking cigarette. Just let's do it then.'

Angela grumbles under her breath that you're like a toddler.

You take pleasure in this comment and start off on the climb again. As you walk, you grind your teeth so much that they make a squeaking noise. You remember how Mary used to say as she washed your teeth for the third time each night that she'd get them squeaky clean. That's what you are. Squeaky, and utterly clean. Nothing marking your presence on this earth: no blights, no slights, just cleanliness coupled with the occasional bout of laziness. Everything else is surface image; the words thought about long and hard, the flowing locks, the shimmering silk shirts, the needle pine green cords. Grab a bottle of Mr Sheen and you'd have it wiped away in a jiffy. You look up at Angela, now lost amongst the panting unfit Americans and camera clicking Japanese. The ponytail is gone now, you notice. It probably annoyed her. Things did that to her. She'd love them, get annoyed by them and get rid of them only to return to them later, full of enthusiasm. She looks part of this landscape, her black jeans and hiking boots, her birch stick – her mother's apparently. There's a blister on your right heel, growing by the minute.

You reach the summit, a few feet one from the other. You ignore the stream of people going into the white chapel.

'You know how high we are from the sea?' she says, her hands on her knees, bent over, out of breath. 'Whoa, that was tough going, eh?'

'You're going to tell me.' You smirk.

'We're almost 2,500 feet above sea level, isn't that incredible?' Angela stands up properly. 'Look,' she points, 'can you see the Bed and Breakfast where we're staying? Isn't this just perfect?'

Before you can reply, she's thrown her arms around you. 'You know, I can't think of another time when I felt so happy. But it's more than that. I'm just... overjoyed. Me and you and this mountain!' She laughs, throwing her head back, her hair tousled, tangled, and beautiful.

'Me, you and this mountain,' you repeat, wanting to touch her hair but instead you look past her.

'We have it all, don't we? You with your dark curls, me with my blonde locks – can't you just picture the beautiful children we'll make?' She's on a roll. 'And if that weren't enough, you've got the steady job; I've handed in my master's thesis.'

You say nothing.

'What do you think, Dirk?'

You think of the view of this place from the window in the bed and breakfast. Everything is linked: the clouds, you can almost touch them, racing with the wind, the islets linked in the sea. You can sense her flailing. Sometimes it's good to let things find their own flow. Your Auntie Sheila would always say that.

There's something, you think, of Sheila in you. Something in you that's happy not to change.

'You know,' she says, 'we should try getting a house before the prices climb too high. A friend of my father's, an investment banker, said Ireland is on the rise. If we buy now it would be such an investment for our future. It'll cement our relationship.'

'Cement,' you echo.

'Well,' she's unsure again, 'maybe cement is too strong. I mean… ' She flicks her hair. 'It's like a commitment.'

'Pity we don't have a camera,' you say. 'It'd be nice to mark this moment, don't you think?'

'We don't need a camera for that.' She leans forward to kiss you.

As you kiss her, you know something has shifted. You shiver.

Angela sits down on a rock, struggling to light a cigarette. 'Besides the bedtime routine,' she says winking at you, 'I also like a cigarette after a bit of a climb. Are you sure you won't have one?'

You lean forward and cup your hands around her cigarette. It catches and she quickly takes a drag. She tilts her head back and blows a wavy line and then a ring of smoke. She's perfect, you think.

'Sure?' she asks.

'Yeah.' And then, feeling you're in a photograph, that you've captured that moment already, you say, watching her enjoy her cigarette, knowing that the opportunity has passed, 'But with a photograph we make sure we know, in years to come, that there was happiness on this summit.'

You look at the mounds of slate, rocks of granite, and the random tufts of grass that are trampled on day after day. Trod upon and trampled on by feet that belonged to people looking for salvation, hoping to find it at the top of a mountain, a mountain that sits in a part of the land that had lost the most people to hunger. A mountain that preached to you of salvation and starvation, starting, so they said, with the Welsh sheep farmer who had become the national saint of the land of saints

111

and scholars. Croagh Patrick of Saint Patrick. And that was what living was about, quelling the hunger and quenching the thirst, you think as you take another drink of water. Quelling and quenching.

'I really need a few whiskeys.'

'We've done the climb, haven't we? And I said we'd go to the pub after it, didn't I? Come on, race you down!' she calls.

She flings her cigarette butt over her shoulder where it lands on some heather.

You stamp out the smouldering cigarette, imagining the blaze out of control, the screams of the tourists as they realise they will spend their last few minutes on this earth trapped on a mountain top on a typically Irish summer's day which had been warmed by the very fire that would kill them.

You stumble, following the flow of her hair down the mountain. There's a chill in your bones.

Last Will to Survive

It was the Wednesday before the Saturday. The morning of a pointless argument. At least that's what remained of it: pointlessness.

'You look like you have a sore head with that face on you,' I said to him. 'I don't think you'll make it into work.'

'No,' he muttered as he crunched some toast, his jaw moving mechanically. He stopped, the toast in mid-air, teeth marks showing on it. 'You're right,' he said sharply. 'It's already past ten. I'd better ring in.'

'Keep on at this rate and you'll lose your job,' I said, wanting to bite my tongue; I wasn't comfortable nagging my son, now a grown man. 'You can't just keep ringing in sick every time you have a hangover.'

He looked at me, his eyes bloodshot. 'I told you. I don't have a hangover.'

'No,' I snapped. 'You didn't tell me. You grunted at me like you've been doing for the past I don't know how many mornings. Grunts and monosyllabic answers is all I get when I try to hold a decent conversation.' I paused. 'I might as well be living on my own.'

'Hmm,' he replied, his legs crossed, a foot jigging. He brushed his palms together and the crumbs fell onto the latest edition of *Hot Press*. He was going out more and more these days and, instead of making me feel happy, it angered me. We no longer talked, we passed each other, the electrics of our anger sometimes meeting.

'Dirk.' I was furious with his *who gives a fuck* attitude.

'I'm on a fucking study day today. For the librarianship diploma you wanted me to do. Happy?' He crossed and uncrossed his legs dramatically and loudly flicked and straightened the pages of the magazine.

'I mean, this is getting pretty unbearable. It's not a hotel. We live together as two adults – you need to be speaking to me and cooking meals now and then. Just because I am your mother doesn't mean I'm your slave.'

He sighed. 'Oh come *on*. Nobody is anybody's slave here.'

'You, young man, need to take a rain check on reality. Life isn't all party, party, party.'

'I'm not feeling the best.'

'A pity about you.'

'Can I not eat my fucking toast in peace?'

'Look at you. Pale, black bags under your eyes and you've lost weight. That's why you don't feel the best. And, oh yes, because you probably drank too much again last night.' I could hear myself speak; I was despicable, but nothing else seemed to move him from that inertia of youth.

'Yeah,' he said. 'I'm working hard, partying hard. Big swinging fucking micky. Show me a guy my age who isn't doing that.'

I sighed. 'With that company you keep, that Dave friend of yours and the others.'

'And?'

'What do you mean, *and?* There's something sleazy about him. I wouldn't trust him as far as I could throw him. You've changed since you met him.'

'How would *you* know he's sleazy? You've only met him a handful of times.'

I could feel my voice shaking as I said it. I'd actually said it aloud. Every mother has a fear that her child will meet someone who is wrong for them and they'll give everything up for them. Dirk's eyes lit up when he talked about him, he wore nice clothes when he went out with him, and he rarely came home before midnight when he was out. He even insisted on buying body spray; he hadn't even done that for Cathy, his first girlfriend. As much as I disliked her, I wished he'd stuck with her, even if it had meant following her to New York. At least I wouldn't have to witness *this*. Dave'd been round a few times and I always shivered when he looked at me, like he was mentally undressing me, a smirk on his face.

'Come on, Horny boy,' he'd say to Dirk. 'We better

skedaddle out of here.'

And Dirk would practically skip down the stairs with a cheery 'See you, Mary, don't wait up.' And they'd stroll down the road, walking with arms linked, or cycling side by side, for all to see, spending Dirk's savings like they weren't going to run out. The next morning, though, would always be the same. He'd grunt at me and if I got a few words out of him I was lucky. I thought that if they were an item, he could have just said it to me, but no, it was grunts and rolling eyes that I got. Even though he'd taken up with Angela out of the blue, the late nights continued. I'd only found out about Angela because I happened to pick up the phone one evening and there she was all girly giggles and politeness. She didn't appear to have matured much either, I thought. There was a gang of them and I wasn't quite sure who was who but there was something I wasn't happy with and it all pointed to Dave.

'You wouldn't know sleazy if it bit you, anyway,' he said, pushing back the chair with a loud scrape.

I'd have to buy new pads for the legs of the chairs; they were scraping the new wood-look-alike lino.

'I want you to stop going out for a while. I don't want you seeing that Dave fella. He's not good for you.'

He slammed his plate down on the table. It cracked in half; a nice, neat crack. My heart pounded. For a second it was me and Sepp, in Germany, arguing about whether we would go to Ireland or stay put in Bamberg. Sepp had wanted to stay where we were. He hurled a bowl at the wall. We stood in silence, watching it smash, the sound of it hitting the wall, the scattering of the pieces. We agreed to leave it to fate, then, that his employers might transfer him if he said he was willing. Within a few years we were being relocated to Dublin, Ireland.

'Not good for me!' Dirk was shouting. 'What's that supposed to mean? Don't think I'm back in school again and you're trying to pick my friends for me. I'm an adult now. You can't tell me who I can and can't see, so don't even try.'

'I can tell you, as a fellow adult, what I think of your friends. And as your mother I want what's best for you. All those parties and gigs aren't doing you any good right now. You need to slow down a bit.'

'What?' he mocked. 'How do you know what's best for me? What sort of a life do you want for me? Not to go out? Not to have friends? I thought you'd be happy I'm going out with Angela. You were certainly happy with her when she didn't want me.'

'Of course I want you to have a life, that's a ridiculous thing to say. Yes, I'm happy you're with Angela. She's the right girl for you, I can tell.'

'Besides, I've taken a rain check on Dave and them, so put that in your pipe and smoke it.' He paused, clenching his fist. 'Actually, Angela doesn't like him. Happy? Are you happy now?' he spat.

I looked at the tears hovering in his eyes. 'Of course I'm not happy that you have to drop a friend because your new girlfriend doesn't like him… But I thought all you lot went out together. To those concerts.' He was staring at me. I had no idea who he met when he went out and Dave hadn't been to the house in a while. I went to put my arms around him.

'Don't fucking dare.'

He pushed me hard and I landed against the kitchen table, pain shooting up the small of my back.

'Dirk,' I started, the tears springing to my eyes.

'If – you – *listened* – to – me.' He spaced the words out, spitting each one at me.

'Well tell me. Tell me now.'

'Butt out,' he shouted. 'I know what this is about. You think I don't but I do. This isn't about any of my friends, is it? It's about me spending my own fucking money that I saved. You want to control me.'

I squeezed my eyes shut, took a deep breath. 'This is about you.'

My throat hurt I was shouting so loudly. He stood, very still, staring at me. I wondered if he had been led astray and owed money. I hadn't even mentioned money. I wished I could hand him his battered Ted and everything would be fine again. *Here, lie down there with Ted and you'll feel better in the morning, Dirk.* He was shouting at me again. My head was pounding, a migraine

116

was coming on.

'Is it really? Because so far it's about you. It's always been about you. Even when Sepp died, it was about you. Never about me. You never thought about how much I wanted a man to look up to, did you? Christ, even when he was fucking alive, it was about you, you, you. I'm surprised he didn't top himself.'

I picked up the two pieces of the plate he'd slammed on the table and brought it to the basin. My face was on fire. I wanted to hit him. I wanted to throw the damned pieces back at him. Instead, I started washing the breakfast dishes, banging them onto the draining board. I cursed Sepp in my mind; he'd got off lightly, he'd escaped this part of parenting.

'That's right,' he shouted at my back. 'Turn your back on me. It's okay when you want to talk, isn't it? But when I suddenly open up, you don't want to know. Isn't that right, Mary?'

'Dirk – '

'It's all about waiting. Having fun, so I am. And still you aren't fucking happy, are you? Isn't Sepp the lucky one now?'

I removed the rubber gloves slowly, suddenly remembering how I'd removed them when my waters had broken, when labour had started on this boy, this man who had a wild look in his eyes and was shouting at me. My hands were shaking and I realised with a shock that I was afraid. Afraid for my son. Afraid of my son.

'Answer me, for fuck's sake, answer me. What the hell more do you want from me? One: I have a job; two: I go out; three: I have a girlfriend. All the boxes are ticked. I'm *living* – fucking *living*.'

'Don't be so stupid.' I could hear the edge of hysteria in my voice. 'Don't be so *ridiculous*. Sit down. Just sit bloody well down and listen to me.'

To my surprise, he sat down. He'd been running his fingers through his hair. His breath was laboured and his cheeks red. He was wringing his hands. Round and round. His legs were crossed and jigging.

'Dirk.' My voice was calmer now. I couldn't panic, I realised. I had to be calm. I sat beside him and reached out for him. He moved his chair further away from me. A picture of him asleep, happiness etched on his face, hugging his beloved Ted, flashed across my mind.

'I don't want anything from you or for you to do anything. Simply, I want you to be happy.'

'That's fine then,' he said, averting his eyes. 'We're finished with this conversation.' He went to stand up.

'No. No, don't walk away. We're not finished. I want to help you if you're not happy.'

He giggled, looking at me, and my heart sank. 'Of course I'm happy. Look at me, what more could I want?' He giggled again.

'That's fine,' I said in as calm a voice as I could muster but a chill ran through me. 'That's fine. But look at yourself in the mirror. Go on, go over to the mirror, there, and look at yourself. You don't *look* fine, Dirk.'

He got up and looked at himself in the mirror. I walked over to him and put my hand on his shoulder. He brushed it away.

'I'm – ' He turned to me as if to speak. His voice faltered.

*

It was the pounding on the door that alarmed me, at first. I was relieved to hear that he'd forgotten his keys. It seemed a reasonable explanation.

'How was the gig?' I asked, rubbing his back. He pushed me away. His face was beyond grey.

'Great,' he replied, his words slurred. 'Shit. We walked out half way. The support was better than the main act.'

His eyes were rolling in his head. I wanted to slap him. I took a deep breath, telling myself it would do no good to get angry with him at nearly three in the morning. 'Just get some sleep, Dirk.'

'Yeah,' he said. 'Got a bit of a headache.'

'Whatever, just get to bed and sleep it off Dirk,' I'd said, trying not to sound annoyed.

And I went back to bed myself and slept like a baby.

On Sunday morning, I got up ready to read my book with my toast and tea when I heard a loud bang from upstairs. I remember I paused, deciding whether I'd go up to him or not. I

118

decided not to. Let him stew in his own hangover, I said to myself. That'll teach him. But something inside me was rattled and I only managed to get to the end of the page I was reading before the ensuing silence unnerved me. I remember my heart started pounding as I walked up the stairs. That must have been my instinct telling me that all was not right. But no instinct could have prepared me for the scene that was Dirk's bedroom.

The thud I'd heard was, by the looks of it, him falling off the bed. He was lying, face down in a pool of vomit on the floor, his trousers around his ankles, wet around the crotch where he'd not made it to the toilet, his faded black underpants stuck to him. His socks with holes in them – *how did I not throw those ones out*, I thought – were still on his feet and a moss-green tee-shirt still on his back. His left hand was clutching the bedspread, the one I'd knitted when I was pregnant with him, and his teddy, his bloody teddy was lying beside his head.

And suddenly I was back in the church again, running up the aisles searching for a nine-year-old him, as I shook his body.

'Dirk!'

He groaned and rolled over fully onto his back. 'Sorry,' he said, stating the obvious. Who intends to make themselves that ill?

'Let's get you cleaned up,' I said, an orderly tone to my voice as I realised – or thought I realised – he was okay. I helped him to his feet and brought him to the bathroom, slowly. He was able to walk, that was good. I turned on the shower, full power.

'Now get into that shower and wake yourself up. Put all the clothes into the laundry basket to be washed. I'll put on a fry for us both. Nothing like a good old-fashioned fry-up to cure a sore head.' And I laughed.

When I think about it now! I laughed as I trotted down the stairs, humming to myself. That would fix him alright. As my toast was now going stale and my tea well cold, it would do no harm to make a complete new breakfast.

I thought I heard him vomiting in the toilet as the sausages spat out their fat and I shook the frying pan, a fury building inside myself. I wasn't quite sure what I was furious at, or why I was furious – at myself for not trying to control his drinking in a more streamlined way? At him for daring to turn up in that state last night? Or furious at my life? For me? For all of it?

He pitched up at the kitchen door. 'Eh... ' he started to speak and leaned against the door, his arm supporting him.

'What?' I snapped, trying to sound angry when I had suddenly turned cold. He was looking at me but his eyes were somewhere else.

'Eh... my headache's gone,' he said, barely audible, and collapsed onto a chair.

'Well, that's good, then,' I replied, my voice sounding stupidly cheerful. 'You'd be wanting something to eat, then.' I divided the sausages between two plates and brought them to the table. 'Mushrooms and eggs on their way. There's toast in the toaster if you want to fetch and butter it.'

'Can't.'

'What do you mean you can't?'

He looked down at his hands shaking furiously. 'I... I drank too much.'

'I can see that. Well, listen, this is a wake-up call for you, right? So, let's learn from it. I'll get the toast.'

'And – '

'And what?' I said, buttering the toast viciously, practically stabbing it with the knife.

'My headache's gone,' he repeated, poking at the sausages with his fork. He started to cut one as I brought the eggs, mushrooms and toast to the table.

'Tea's ready. Will I be mammy and pour?'

'I took tablets.'

I bit into the toast, gobbling it, not wanting to look at him, not wanting to hear what he was saying. He was mumbling, a lot of it nonsensical.

'I took a lot of tablets. Crunched them. Crunched the tablets.'

Tablets, he said. He'd taken tablets.

'What tablets? At the gig? A party?'

He put a piece of sausage in his mouth. He was chewing it like it was poison. I took a gulp of tea, banging the mug down on the table.

'What kind of tablets?'

'No,' he said. 'At home.'

'At home? At the party? You took tablets there *and* at home? Which is it?' I could feel the tears beginning to spring. He could have taken anything. Maybe he was already taking things – regularly – and I just hadn't noticed. Jesus Christ. He was moody. He'd lost weight. I looked at him out of the corner of my eye, my heart was thundering in my chest. He reached into his dressing gown pocket and handed me the box of paracetamol.

'Oh, thank God, Dirk,' I said, the tears now flowing. 'I thought you'd taken ecstasy or something like that. Thank God!'

He looked at me, his face grim. He was shaking his head.

'What?' I peered inside the box. There were a handful of tablets left.

'I ate them,' he said, a half-smile, half-grimace on his face.

I looked at him; there was a whirring noise in my ears. I wanted him to start laughing, and shout April Fool!

'I took tablets,' he repeated.

I reached for *The Which Guide to Family Health*, one of those books you have for years. You rarely consult it and, when you do, you need an answer, which of course it doesn't have. I scanned the contents. Part four was 'Accidents and First Aid'. I flicked to page 175, my hands shaking. My eyes raced through the headings: 'avoiding shock', *flick, flick, flick*, 'childbirth', *flick*, 'epilepsy', *flick*. And there it was. 'Poisoning'. I cleared my throat.

'There's a section here on poisoning,' I said, as Dirk looked at me, expressionless.

I started reading aloud. 'Check the labels of any bottles or containers and make sure that these go with him to the hospital.'

'When the fuck was that published?' he slurred. 'Nineteen seventy bloody five? It's out of date, for God's sake.'

Stupidly I started flicking to the start of the book, checking. It was published in 1980. He wasn't far out. Then suddenly I remembered the article I'd read the other week about the dangers of accidental overdoses. My heart sank as I tried to remember when the last time was that I'd bought a family box of painkillers. A few weeks ago? And how many had I taken since then? No idea. A handful, probably. He didn't even like taking tablets, or so he always said. I looked inside again. Definitely not many left. That article had said that in cases of overdoses you had to get them to the hospital within a certain time – Christ, what was it? A day? A few hours? – I knew it wasn't long.

'Okay,' I said loudly, my heart working overtime. 'Okay. Now just sit here. Sit here and have some tea. Don't move.'

He rested his cheek on the kitchen table, his eyelids fluttering.

I went into the hall, breathing deeply, counting to ten. I dialled 999.

'My son has accidentally taken too many painkillers,' I said on the third ring when they picked up. My voice was shaking. My hands were like ice. I was shivering.

'I don't know when,' I replied feebly. 'Yes, I think within the last twelve hours. I can take him, I don't need an ambulance. Okay. No. I didn't mean to ring emergencies. Sorry. So I take him to the nearest hospital? Now?'

*

I wore a red coat. Although it was knee-length, it didn't touch my knees as the baby that was once Dirk Horn sat inside me the last time I wore it and stretched it out of all proportion. I stroked the arm of it and shivered. I looked at my reflection in the mirror. There was a cold look about my face, despite the unusual warm September weather. Strands of my hair escaped out of my hand-crocheted hat, the one I'd worn the day my Sepp asked me to marry him – the Sepp I'd moved from his country to mine with a stroke of that magic wand called love. Despite the strain, in a strange way I looked even beautiful. I pulled on my matching red leather gloves and wiggled my fingers before taking them off; it wasn't near cold enough to need gloves. I was now ready to turn on the house alarm before

122

driving to the same hospital where I kissed Sepp his last goodbye.

I drove with Dirk in the front seat vomiting into an orange *Super Crazy Prices* bag that rustled every time the vomit hit the bottom of it. Although by now he was gagging. There didn't seem to be anything left to vomit. And then he fell asleep, groaning. The article had said it was a hard death, death by liver poisoning. Listening to him groaning on and off I wondered if he were in pain. Was his liver dying already? Was I losing him? When I broke through a red light and got beeped at I realised that there was nothing I could do. I was doing the best. That was all I could do. That was all any mother can do. Her best.

When we got to the hospital he pulled from his coat pocket a sealed envelope with my name scrawled in what was unmistakably his drunken writing across the front. We walked together, like an elderly couple, his arm around my shoulder, supporting himself, into emergencies.

They asked how many he'd taken, had he had anything else – that was the part we were unsure of, he was nodding then shaking his head, I began to wonder if he really was aware of what was going on – and when had he taken the tablets. My blood ran cold as soon as they'd lain him down on the bed. This was no accident. I kissed his cheek and closed the curtain, taking a deep breath.

As I walked away from the section where he lay, a nun caught my arm. 'Are you okay?' she asked. 'This wasn't your fault. Young people, you know, they're selfish.'

'Yes, yes,' I replied, eager to escape.

I kept walking until I was outside. Had I looked behind me, I would have seen the nun go in to Dirk. It felt cold, although it wasn't. I opened the envelope. I was shaking. I sat on the edge of a wall. *My son has tried to take his own life.* The tears came with a deep sense of shame, of guilt, of doubt. Yes, of course I had tried my best – who doesn't? – but that hadn't been enough. My best had not been enough for my only child. I had to call Sheila. Oh God, those worries I had. We'd laughed them off but somewhere I *really* knew everything was falling. I had it in my head that it was going to be a lengthy note with a convoluted explanation, typical of Dirk. It wasn't. It was crumpled, barely legible, and full of arrogant news-reel statements. In a strange way, its silliness gave me comfort, like Dirk's giggle. Not quite appropriate. It struck me that his attempt was not an attempt at all. In fact, he hadn't really tried to take his own life; but it was a statement of loss, of vulnerability. A stupid drunken summation of his life. I put it back in the envelope.

I stood up and watched the cars roaming the car park for spaces. It was a Sunday morning and already the place was packed. I stood there for a few minutes, counting the cars, while in the back of my mind the very real thought that Dirk could die sat like the proverbial white elephant. And I thought, then, for the first time in years, of the baby that I'd lost. *Flora Maria.* The baby that was not destined to survive. I closed my eyes momentarily and walked back into the hospital.

'I am his mother,' I said in the loudest voice I could manage as I looked at Dirk. He was groaning, bile rolling down his chin, one of those stupid sky blue transparent gowns on him. The nurse was trying to shove tubes down his throat. I thought about how he squirmed in my belly in tune to the clacking of the needles as I knitted his patchwork bedspread. It was in the washing machine, now, washing out the vomit; his last will to survive.

'Mrs Horn. Walk with me,' Doctor O'Brien said, nodding at the nurse.

I kissed Dirk's cheek. He'd fallen unconscious again.

'Tell me about your son. His lifestyle. His alcohol consumption. Does he take recreational drugs? I know you've given a lot of information – useful stuff that we don't always get, so that's good – but there may be more things. Anything you can think he might have taken, what he's eaten, what he did last night?'

And I spoke, like a robot, about Dirk in the third person, like you'd speak about a character in a film. It felt like that. It felt even worse than the day I brought Sepp into the same hospital. And the picture I painted of Dirk didn't even sound like my son. It was a stranger with whom I had – I realised – spent the last few years since we lost Sepp, observing but not knowing. Hearing but not listening. As I spoke I began to cry. Dirk's story didn't sound like a happy one. It sounded like a lonely one.

Doctor O'Brien spoke. 'In a very strange turnabout, Mrs Horn, young Dirk may be lucky. We've pumped his stomach, administered the antidote, all within 12 hours of the overdose which means – '

'Oh, yes, I forgot to give you this box,' I said, untangling it from Dirk's envelope. 'It was probably three quarters full, I'd say.'

I watched his face as he looked at the label. 'Right,' he said. 'Well, he might have ingested what? Sixty? Maybe more? That's a high number.'

'Excuse us!' yelled a junior doctor and a nurse as they whizzed past us with a patient on a trolley.

Doctor O'Brien and I squashed ourselves against the wall.

'Isn't there anywhere quiet we could go?' I asked.

'Afraid not,' he said, looking at his beeper which had started to sound. 'I'm also afraid,' he said, 'that I've got to go to another emergency.' He raised his eyebrows. 'Stay with me and we can continue talking.'

'So, doctor, is it okay, do you think?'

He stopped walking and, placing an authoritative hand on my shoulder, said, 'I will be able to give you the proper prognosis. Let me explain in the best way I can. You see in a normal, healthy adult, alcohol taken with a paracetamol overdose doesn't increase any injury caused to the liver. In fact, as the two compounds compete for the same metabolic pathways, there may be a protective effect from the alcohol. That's something that a lot of medics are unaware of but, unfortunately, this is my speciality.'

I watched his face. He was ashamed to be working as a doctor trying to save the lives of those who wanted nothing more than to end their lives. I was aware of a bead of sweat resting on my forehead. I felt stifled, suddenly. He started walking again, a quick pace, every now and then glancing at his beeper as he gave his lecture.

'So, despite the positives, we still do not know the final outcome, Mrs Horn. Hepatic necrosis can begin to develop after 24 hours and can progress to acute liver failure. We're on the lookout for possible renal failure, taking urine samples, monitoring output and analysing his blood glucose levels and, until we know he's in the clear, it's nil by mouth for him, which is why we've got him on a drip.' He lowered his voice as he spoke again. 'I know it's a mine of information for you to take in but I believe in educating my patients.'

'Oh, just call me Mary, just call me Mary. I haven't been a missus since he died.' And it was then the tears came fast and furious.

'I see this all the time,' he said, a condescending tone to his voice.

'No,' I said, pulling myself together. 'No, not this family, you don't, doctor. I've been diagnosed with cancer, not given long to live and my boy, who may or may not be dead tomorrow or the next day, has no idea. He lost his father at just sixteen. And in this very hospital too. So no. You do *not* see this all the time.'

He looked, for once, as if he were lost for words. He stopped and shook his head.

'I'm so sorry, Mary. I am so sorry for you and I am very, very sorry for Dirk. I'll leave you with this Garda here, now.'

'What?'

'You might not be aware but suicide is a criminal offence. They have to take a statement.'

'Criminal?'

'Don't worry. Just say it was accidental.'

'Oh.'

'And as soon as we know how he gets on over the next few days, if he's okay, Dirk will be transferred – on medical and psychiatric grounds because he has attempted suicide – to our psychiatric ward.'

I could feel my head spinning. A psychiatric ward?

'Give me back my son and I will make him better myself. This is a mistake.' The words sprang out of my mouth before I could rein them back in.

'It's not a question of making him better, Mary. It's about

how you can help him to help himself.' He started walking again. 'Maybe he had an operation, if you want.'

'An operation?'

'You don't *have* to tell anybody that your son tried to commit suicide.' He paused, cocking his head to one side. 'Go to him and Eithne will take care of you. Now, I'm afraid I'm in here,' he said, indicating a cubicle.

I squeezed my hat in my hands, wringing it out as if it were dripping wet. 'Just tell me he's okay,' I whispered into the air as the curtain was drawn shut.

Possessions

The Ward Sister waved the crucifix at him like a loaded gun. It swung on an overly-long silver chain, glinting with the little sunlight that radiated through old and worn beige blinds. Her voice was harsh, croaky.

'Look what you've done to yourself! Is this how you thank your parents for bringing you into this world? Try to leave it? It's a sin, you know, a mortal sin.'

Time after time it was the anger that came first. Anger at the messiness and downright *un-necessary-ness* of it all.

She could tell he wanted to say something, to make a sound, an objection of sorts. He tried to move but the drips attached to his right arm stopped him and, instead of words, groans came from his mouth. He began to heave.

'Mother of God, there's no hope. Just look at him.'

She blessed herself, wiping away her disgust. She wiggled her toes inside their 50-denier flesh coloured tights and picked up the notes from the locker. A self-admittance with his mother at twenty past twelve in the afternoon. She shook her head. It was probably the mother he was trying to get away from. She sighed. Another professional: a librarian from a nice part of town. One Dirk Horn. The Gardaí had come and gone: the mother in tears, the son unconscious. She'd signed to say it was a mistake, he hadn't wanted to, he *couldn't have* wanted to kill himself. They nodded, embarrassed at the legal intrusion, saying they'd be back in the morning to talk to him. If he lived, that was.

His possessions sat in a transparent plastic bag to be taken to the psychiatric ward when he was stabilised. They were listed in a row. Probably penned by one of the aides, judging by the neat handwriting:

one pair of blue jeans

one navy heavy cotton hooded jumper

128

one white tee-shirt
one pair of grey underpants
one pair of white socks
one right and one left of black runners
one wrist-watch with a worn tan leather strap
no valuables on person

At moments like this she found the movements of Sunday morning A&E depressing. But still, she stayed. Still, there was hope to be found in between the drunken people screaming abuse at staff, shouts for doctors and the sound of the trolleys racing, bringing bodies to beds, wards, slots in the morgue. She stared at a fifty-something-year-old woman gyrating against a soft drinks machine. *Yeah baby* she screamed, laughing loudly, oblivious to the dried blood on her face, escaped from a blow to the head. Curtains opened and closed, cries of fears and anger rose above the clang of equipment. But still, there were rosters to be organised, wards to be filled, beds to be emptied. And soon Dirk would open his eyes to the realisation that it was still 1992, still the same weekend that he'd tried to leave behind.

*

Flashes of silver, voices, footsteps seeped into his consciousness. Perhaps he hadn't made it home last night. Maybe he was tripping into the darkness.

But no, actually.

Cold fear mixed with shame slithered over him. He opened his eyes, marginally. Dirk tried to sit up. His eyelids felt so heavy. His head hung forward. One word fluttered like a broken butterfly across his consciousness: failure.

'Don't close your eyes, Kirk.'

A voice to one side of him spoke. As he felt her warm hand take his pulse gently, her soft voice and touch merged with the whiteness of her uniform and blonde hair. She was his light, like he had once been for his father. But now, in his head, there were more words than hers, streams of them, flowing, full of feelings.

His mother told him his name meant *ruler of the people*.

Neigh, he used to say as a child when he was nervous. *Neigh*. It gave him strength, this pretence that he was a leader bareback on a horse. It made him become the words put upon him: special; precious.

And now as the nurse whispered each beat of his pulse, in his mind he saw what had not happened. What, perhaps, had he logically thought of it, he would have liked to happen: a picture of his body at sea, floating, the sparkle of the sun as it bounced, at peace. And in his head there was a silence like he'd never heard before, like when his ears used to pop as a child up high in the mountains and the world suddenly seemed a more bearable place. Beauty. Softness. Warmth. Light.

*

'What? What's he saying? Kirk?'

'His name. It's Dirk. With a *D*. Read the chart, woman, read the chart!'

She clutched the chart to her chest. These nurses would soon learn the ropes. No time could be wasted with patients like these.

There were ripples of sweat on Dirk's skin. The nurse had a palm pressed against his forehead. He strained against the pressure, groaning. His legs convulsed. He struggled to breathe. He was panicking.

'Have his stomach pumped and we'll transfer him to Saint Marcella's Ward. Doctor O'Brien is on his way to administer Parvolex.'

She sneaked a smile.

This was good. He was fighting.

Girl, Aged 18

She projects herself onto a future self, insisting she's 19 already. I make a mark in the margins; this is something to watch for, expectations of greatness at 19, happiness even. She walked into the hospital and asked to be admitted to a *mental ward.* She appeared to be intoxicated. On blood analysis traces of barbiturates, sleeping tablets and alcohol were found. She claims she said she'd taken an overdose but that nobody responded and instead forced her onto a bed and stuck needles into her.

'They strapped me down,' she says. 'All I needed was a mental ward but they shoved needles into me, taking *my blood* away from me without my permission. It's like I'm in some sort of horror film.'

I nod, looking at the sheen in her dark brown hair, long, to her waist. It's been combed. Her skin is fresh though her eyes have dark circles around them. She looks like a girl who's had too much of a good night, except for the hospital gown, of course. She slept well, her chart notes, although became aggressive when woken at 5am for blood tests. It's amazing, really, I think with a smile, to see her so *well.*

'See?' she says to me, eyebrows raised, challenging. 'Nobody *listens* unless there's something in it for them.'

She does have a point. 'That's how you perceive it.'

My voice is calm and even, an edge of authority to it. I chew the end of my pen and think of the song 'This Train' by Sister Rosetta Tharpe. My mother used to play her records when I was a toddler in the late fifties, records sent over by an uncle I never met. He lived far away, she'd say with sadness, in a city called Philadelphia. She brought me there, once, as an older boy of about ten. We buried him in a coffin painted white. She put a red rose on it as it disappeared down beneath clumps of mud. She cried as the men covered the coffin, flecks of dry earth splattering. There were five people at the funeral including us. She talked of rain, afterwards, and how Uncle Tommy never found a wife because he loved Rosetta too much. 'Never,' she said, 'love your idol too much.'

I nodded, tears nearing the surface, fearful because of the cross look in her eyes, shameful because I didn't understand what she wanted me to say. She took a suitcase with Tommy's belongings and from it she gave me a book, Freud's *Interpretation of Dreams*. Tommy, she explained, would have wanted you to read this. Even at ten, or almost eleven by that stage, it felt like a burden. But read it I did, and understand it I did and by sixteen I had my life's career mapped out.

'See?' the girl Ita says.

I laugh. 'Sorry.' I apologise, thinking maybe I should just go home. It is the tenth anniversary of my mother's death. No matter how much I try to deny it, the day she died creeps up on me every year, evident in my moods and concentration. I should just cross it out on my calendar. Obliterate that day, 21st September.

'What were you running away from, Ita?' I ask, my focus returning.

She shifts on the grey plastic chair, pulls her right leg up and rests it on her left leg at an angle. She shrugs.

I swing back on my chair, my heart skipping a beat. It's been doing that a lot, recently. The doctor tried to convince me I had developed arrhythmia. *Que sera, sera.* My mother used to sing when she bathed me. Your path is set out before you. I want to say this to these young men and women who appear before me. *Just relax. What will be, will be.* But I know they won't understand. They believe destiny is to go on trying to change it; stuffing themselves with tablets and drink, lacerating their soft skin, trying to get somewhere other than where they are. And some day they just might do that.

'You might fall,' she says.

There's distrust in her eyes. I let the chair go and wobble as it settles down flat. I shrug. She bites the nail of her left thumb. Both thumbnails are bitten but her fingernails are long and elegantly shaped.

'I dunno.' She doesn't look at me.

I spread my hands out flat on the table. I want to see her nails. I want to see if they are evenly and homogenously shaped.

'Everything,' she says, catching her breath. 'Everything.' She raises her voice.

'Like what?' I ask. I write *everything* on the paper. I look at my watch and note the time.

'Like everything.' She wants to hate me, I can see how she's gearing herself up into believing that I, too, am to blame.

'Okay,' I reply. 'Okay. And do you think it worked? Or is this what you wanted? You said you wanted this, didn't you? You asked for a mental ward.'

She shakes her head. 'You know what I want, what I really want?'

'I haven't a notion. But I hope you do.' I smile. There is something open about her, suddenly. There is a scent of roses in the air.

'I just want to *be*,' she says, triumphantly. 'That's all, nothing much.' She spreads her hands on the table. I try to draw her nails; they are just perfectly manicured. Her thumbs are like intruders. She has piano fingers; I wonder if she plays.

I smile again, the echo of my heartbeat in my ears. 'Such simple desires, Ita. Surely they don't require violence to be achieved. I mean what you did to your body.'

'No... ' She hesitates. 'But, like I said, nobody listens. And you know what?' She bangs a fist on the table. 'You know what? *This* got them listening, didn't it?'

It saddens me, deeply, to hear comments like this. Not many patients make them, of course; not many have such insight as Ita. Most are so angry they can barely articulate a sentence. Ita is different. She takes a miniature Anaïs Anaïs perfume from somewhere behind her back. I don't even ask how she's managed to have held on to it. It looks like glass though you can cut yourself with plastic, too. She gently dabs each wrist with it.

'I couldn't do this if I'd self-harmed,' she says, grinning.

'True,' I reply.

'Did you *see* that girl's arms?' she says leaning forward. 'Jesus!

133

I couldn't do that – could you imagine the blood?'

I shake my head.

'I would just fucking faint or something. She says it's like a drug, you know?'

I shake my head.

'I'll be back here, like her. You'll sign me out but I'll be back again, you know that, don't you?'

'What?' I clear my throat. This isn't the first time this has happened, where I've somehow lost the thread in a session. There are just over four minutes left of it.

'I will. That's what they're all saying out there.'

'And you believe them?'

She looks down at her lap. My heart jumps again. There's a second when I want to reach out and take the hand that has crept back onto the table. I want to stroke it, to comfort her. I count to seventy-three in my head. I am nearly sure I can smell roses. Or maybe it's chrysanthemums. That's what my mother had at her funeral. White ones; she left instructions in the note penned with Tommy's old fountain pen, an out of character flourishing 'y' in the script.

Ita looks up. She's crying.

'All I ever wanted to be was a singer,' she says wiping the tears with the back of her hand. She sniffs loudly, her face red. Her hands are shaking. 'Beautiful like my mother. She died, you know? I was only a fucking kid.'

'Then sing,' I say. I write *Not happy with career choice* in her notes. And beside it I write *psychosis,* adding a question mark beside the word *mother.* I take a deep breath.

She slowly closes the perfume bottle and pushes it towards me. I take it and smell its floral scent.

Then she sings.

She sings the most beautiful rendition of *Cry Me A River* I have ever heard.

The room is filled with the sadness of dying flowers. Mother would have wept.

Maladies

This is the one thing you're not meant to fail at. Like, you want to do things right and this *act* (it is an act, it's a stepping-out-of-yourself-and-your-world) is the way you'll finally, finally be a *success*. You've tried so many things, done as your mam told you – practise and try real hard. But none of it's worked.

You're a criminal. And soon you'll be a repeat offender. Aren't you in a mental ward, full of failed suicides? Haven't you got to repeat to succeed? Durkheim, a well-known French sociologist once said that suicide was an individual act for which the collective had responsibility. That is, according to this old-timer who's been here loads of times. It's a pity she can't get it right, you think to yourself. Bullshit. And then you turn away with the look she gives you. And you think that nobody coming into Saint Marcella's Ward can possibly give a toss about society.

*

There aren't any words to describe the whirlwind of smoke that sucks you down. Smoke like the cigarettes or the drink or the whatever it is that took your fancy. And then. Then you can't describe the shame you feel afterwards. It's worse than the loneliness.

It'd make you want to do it again.

And that's what it is. All of it. An escape. You've said it so many times they just roll their eyes at you. How can you say you swallowed half a box of sweet little pink sleeping tablets and drank an entire bottle of gin *just* to escape? Not just a normal gin and tonic – that wouldn't have done for you. You had it neat.

Gin, your Dad said, is a depressant. It won't do you any good, he said. It bloody well will, you retorted, deciding, finally

135

deciding, and glad of a decision, that you'd had it. Try beer, or even wine like the ladies, he suggested. It's cheaper. But wine wouldn't do, you thought, it would just make your lips all purple, highlight the dry lines like crevices. The drink of choice had to be clear like your conscience, clear, smart, effective. Like the *act* of your life.

*

A new guy came in late this morning. You wander into his room. You look at his name on his chart. It hangs on a bedrail, like many of the guys in here once hung from a rope. The name sounds German. You watch his eyes flutter and close, the odd groan from his lips. You decide to keep a close eye on this one.

You tell Nurse that you'll watch out for him. She gives you one of those looks and makes a note on your chart which she takes away. You'll be called in for another session with the psychiatrist who wants to label you. He's been bouncing the idea of voices off you, trying to convince you that the voices told you to do it.

No, you insist. Only one voice. You tell him again. Just one. Mine. In my head.

He asks, again, if it sounded or does it sound, different to your own voice. Like your mam's, for instance.

No.

You feel like grabbing him by his starched collar. Did you not hear me? No, it didn't. It was a voice, a thought, just like any other. Just like, I'll have cornflakes for breakfast this morning. Just like the fact that my mam is dead. Stone dead.

He nods. He avoids your eyes. He pretends to write something but you can tell from the way the fountain pen moves across the page that he's doodling.

You wonder if you should just make things easier for him, for them. Just say that the voices made you. And swallow the pills they so desperately want to prescribe.

They'll make you feel better, he says. By way of encouragement, he raises his eyebrows.

The German guy is fully awake. And he's not bad, either. You feel conscious of your feet inside paper slippers. You'd give anything, just now, for a nice pair of heels. A bit of a click. A hint of a clack.

'Hey,' you finally say.

He nods, looks away.

You follow his gaze to the curtains.

That's the thing about hospital curtains. They're just hideous. If you were a curtain in a hospital you'd have definitely topped yourself long ago. There'd be none of this couple of dozen tablets lark, there'd be a couple of hundred to do the job right.

They're short of beds in public wards, so they say. But he's one in a room of six beds and you're sharing a room with just three others, now. Eilís has been taken away after biting the Ward Sister – and drawing blood – last night when all she wanted to do was take her temperature. You lay underneath the light sheet, unsure whether you were laughing at the screams or crying because of them. It's like that. You just don't know how to be feeling. But when you say that to any of them they look at you and nod, like you've just said something that will scar you for life. It's like you've just confirmed their worst suspicions about you, like you are so clever you are mad.

'Hey,' the German finally says.

You stand at the edge of the bed. 'I'm going up to the communal area.'

'Is it far?'

You laugh. 'Like, two doors up.'

'The corridor?'

'The doors out of here are locked. You know that, right?'

He nods, stands up. He's wearing black jeans and furry grey slippers.

'The doors of the corridor, I mean,' you explain. 'It's for our *safety*.'

Instead of laughing he looks like he's about to cry.

'Oh come on, it's not that bad.'

You smile. He looks at you, his face blank.

137

'They stood guard while I had the first fucking shower in days,' he says.

'They do that.' You shrug. 'Did he stand with his back to you with the door open?'

He nods.

'They do that.' And you're like a pro. 'First time?'

He nods. 'You?'

'Yeah. Probably not the last, though.' You shiver suddenly.

He frowns, takes a step back from you.

'What?' you say. 'You're not going to keep trying?'

He shakes his head.

'No?' you laugh again. 'That's what you say now. You're in shock still. It's the shame, isn't it?'

He shrugs.

'Don't say it's not. We're all the same in here. And most of us will be back. A French sociologist said so, actually. He used statistics.' You wiggle your toes, pretending they're inside patent sandals with peep-toes. Of course you're clever, you remind yourself. You've always been clever.

'What statistics?'

'The studies on suicide. It's just life.' You look away, hiding your blushing face.

But he follows you.

The communal area has tables and chairs: brown pvc which looks like wood. There are two sofas, four armchairs and a TV which seems to show nothing but news and cartoons. There are no nails, no sharp bits. Everything is rounded, smooth, like death.

He stands with his hands in fists in his pockets. 'So… ' he says and smiles.

'Ita,' you say holding out your hand.

'Dirk,' he replies. 'Dirk with a D and not Kirk with a K.' He laughs loudly.

'Dirk,' you repeat, 'from Dublin?'

He nods.

You smile. 'Like me.' You hold out your hand. 'Come on, let's watch Mickey Mouse.'

No unhappiness in life necessarily makes you kill yourself unless you're already inclined. Like your dad used to say *drink in, truth out*. Whatever is in there is going to come out.

Later, you'll ask Dirk why he did it and he'll tell you it was because of a girl. Or a guy. You'll look at his neck, see the bruises and marks; he won't let you touch it but he'll cry. Cry with the shame. Or maybe he'll be different from the other guys. Maybe he took tablets, like you. Maybe he's the sensitive type. You'll tell him it's okay, that it's all okay, you understand.

Later, Dirk will ask you why you did it and you'll cry, too. You'll tell him you were abused (that's what he'll expect) and he'll put his arm around you, just one arm so he shows he's not being intrusive. And you'll lean your head on his shoulder while your cries subside. You'll both feel better. You'll sleep, separately, in the foetal position. Maybe even you'll snore.

Everyone needs to hear why. With little white lies that make sense of the void.

Red Girl

How I love those candy cigarettes.

School day afternoons are spent in front of the full-length mirror of the bedroom Dad now calls his, my uniform hiked up at the waist. The top three buttons of my shirt are open and my dark blonde hair's backcombed. On my lips I have a streak of red lipstick from a black tube that I found buried at the bottom of a handbag which beckoned with its sparkles. And I puff on the brittle chalky stick, dragging the air into my lungs, wondering what it was that Mam had felt when she'd sucked in the air – the hollows of her cheeks showing – and coughed so violently she spat blood.

I pretend she's with me, wearing a fancy dress. She smiles broadly, not caring about her yellow teeth. I smell the air that used to be where she'd stood: sweet, like the flowers at her funeral, mixed with headiness of smoke.

I open my eyes wide and then narrow them, seeing her behind me, hands on my shoulders, teaching me.

'That's it,' she says, 'a nice big deep breath. See?' And she leans down and whispers in my ear. 'See, Ita? Feel that lift in you?'

I nod. 'Oh yeah,' and I turn to touch her hand but she's gone and I know now, what it was she felt, what it was that kept her sucking until she could suck no more.

I feel, at ten, maybe I'm dying like her. I hold my breath and count, unable to keep my eyes closed as my chest feels like it's going to burst. I watch my face go redder, the veins beside my eyes bursting out of my face. And then I let go, head spinning. I've run out of candy cigarettes so I blow my lemon bubble gum bigger and bigger until it pops and sticks to the mirror. I rub the slight stain it leaves when I peel it off to chew it again.

I'm bored.

I root through Mam's drawers, pull out panties. Red, off-white, dirty-white-grey, black; and slips like dresses. Then I hover over the shiny black ones that I remember seeing her in. She'd been running from the bathroom to the bedroom, rushing so she'd be on time for the weekly night in the pub with Dad.

'What?' she frowned at me, cigarette burning in her hand, the panties tight around her thighs. 'I'm in a hurry.'

I shrugged, turning back to my Barbie.

'You'll be good when we're gone, now, won't you?'

I shrugged again.

'Is that all you can do? Shrug?' she snapped, peering around the doorway a second later, fixing her favourite dress, purple velvet. But her eyes smiled. Sparkles of purple just beneath her plucked eyebrows. They were little lines now, like quarter moons, like her life was already spent.

'You look like a princess,' I said, thinking of the princesses who'd floated in my dreams for years.

She laughed. 'And you're the daughter of a princess so you must be a… little princess.'

My tummy went fuzzy I felt so happy. I was mesmerised as she painted her face. She opened her mouth and traced its shape slowly with the sharp purple pencil then coloured the fleshy bits in with lipstick. She smacked her lips together and smiled. Taking a sparkling fluffy puff from her cerise pink make-up bag, she dabbed her cheeks then passed it over her forehead and nose. She sneezed.

'Aren't you tired?' she said, turning.

'I was watching you putting on your face.'

'And I was watching you,' she smiled as she ruffled my hair. 'Well?' She cocked her head to one side.

'You're a queen, now,' I said.

She kissed my forehead. I could feel a perfect purple imprint of her lips on me. 'Oops.' She laughed and licked her thumb, rubbing the imprint away.

That night I held my hand on the spot where she kissed me.

I feel the material of her black panties between my fingers and smile, hearing the smack of her lips on my forehead. I roll *My*

141

Little Pony panties off like they are Plasticine, letting them sit on the floor, ownerless. I step into her black ones. They're slippy on my skin. I fasten a purple pink belt around my middle to stop them falling down.

'*You,*' I giggle, 'are a real princess.' I wiggle, watching my reflection, waving my arms in the air and fluttering my eyelashes.

My stomach rumbles; I've only had a packet of Monster Munch since school. The bread has green fluffy bits on it again and there's no ham left in the fridge. I think Dad's on a late shift at the ice-cream factory and I wonder if he's left any coins on the mantelpiece for me to buy a bag of chips.

I mime a Madonna song to the mirror and dance, laughing, forgetting about my sore stomach, forgetting that Mam is gone, gone, gone.

'What the fuck do you think you're doing?'

Dad stares as he spits the words out. Mam was gone and I, the reason he married her, was growing into her, waiting to becoming a Mam-of-one with lank blonde-grey hair, on 30-a-day, bound for death by lung cancer. I look at my toenails, the chipped red nail varnish glowing, my face burns, the sweet taste of the gum in my mouth now bitter.

*

I bought the first pair of shoes with my babysitting money: they called me. If the pair of red killer heels with *Lady Luck* written on the undersoles was going to bring me anything it would be luck. I bought a new black satin bra and panties set that day as well. I'd worn only black underwear since Dad had stuffed three black bin bags full of Mam's clothes and left them for the bin men to collect.

'You can't put her stuff in with the rubbish,' I screamed that day, five years ago. I kept picturing carrot peels and rotten tomatoes mixed with the satin and silk, wishing I wasn't crying, wishing I was strong. I was glad I'd put away her remnants: a purple pencil, a lipstick, a pink hanky and a pair of turquoise wedge sandals, barely worn.

Dad's lips were tight and closed. His face was set as he filled the bags.

'I'll grow into them,' I shouted.

'She's not coming back.' He took a breath and it sounded like he had a catch in his voice. 'So don't *you* go trying to make it any better.'

I shivered in bed, that night, convinced I would choke on my tears.

I prayed hard that my body would grow fast into that of a woman so that he'd regret throwing her clothes away.

I'd be beautiful wearing her turquoise wedges. I'd wear black satin and never let anyone throw my things away. Dad had tried to rub her out like a bad pencil drawing. I wouldn't disappoint: I wouldn't just look like her, I'd be better than her.

*

My best friend Maeve and I would hop on the bus into town. We were bored with cigarettes and kisses behind the bicycle shed at school. My purple lip liner ran out so I bought a red one. And new red lipstick. Purple was for bishops and tabernacles, I told Maeve. Red was for ladies. We fell about the place laughing at weekends as I strutted around in those *Lady Luck* heels and danced to Billy Idol without falling over.

In town, Maeve and I would sit at the bar of the Brassiere Lounge. Nobody asked for ID. We'd order a Coke between us because we knew within ten minutes some guy with strands of hair over his bald bit would smile and nod. We looked at least eighteen with the make-up that we'd perfected.

'West Coast Cooler,' we'd say in unison.

We'd wear Maeve's Mam's blouses with our jeans and heels. We'd spend ages trying them on, the radio blaring behind us: Erasure, The Thompson Twins, Kate Bush.

Maeve's mam thought it was funny. 'What happened to playing skipping or whatever?' she'd ask us.

And we'd cry laughing.

'Mam!' Maeve would say.

'Mrs Flynn,' I'd say, 'nobody plays skipping any more.'

'I don't want you two getting into any trouble, mind.'

'Yaw, yaw,' Maeve would reply.

'Whatever poor lad thinks you're from a posh part of Dublin will have a wake-up call when that accent slips,' she said sharply. 'You should never be ashamed of where you're from.'

A turquoise blouse was particularly flattering on me with my dark blonde hair, a pair of tight stonewashed denim jeans and my red *Lady Lucks*. The outfit was complemented by mixing red and pink shadow with night-black mascara. A peacock green vest with a short black skirt looked ace on black-haired Maeve, teamed with glittering green eye-shadow and a frosted pink lipstick.

That was the day we met Patsy McDermott.

We were at our usual spot at the bar. Maeve kept crossing and uncrossing her legs, not used to the tight skirt.

'Jaysus, would ya stop?' I said.

'It's too short,' she hissed.

'For fuck sake,' I said as I splayed my legs like a guy.

That set her off.

'You,' she said, pausing to have a suck of Coke. 'You're a mad thing.'

'Takes one to know one.' I blew a bubble at her.

'Ladies,' Patsy said, tipping his mink grey hat to each of us. He had a smile like one of those fellas from Hollywood. All white and perfect like he'd chewed some minty gum all his life.

'Howya,' I said.

'Hello, sir,' said Maeve.

I rolled my eyes at her. She just shrugged.

'Can I offer you two beautiful ladies a drink?'

His eyes started at the tops of our heads and slowly travelled to our feet. Maeve's shoe fell from her crossed leg. He bent down and picked it up, looking her right in the eye and smiling.

'Thanks,' she said, blushing.

'West Coast Cooler,' we said.

'Two West Coasts it is, so,' he said.

He looked like he was from the country with his rosy cheeks and farmer's hands, big and square and rough. But his nails were shaped and perfectly clean, like he'd scrubbed them with a

144

brand new nail brush that morning. But he didn't just want to buy us drinks and chat. Patsy wanted to give us something. Patsy was the manager of an under-21 rugby team with some of the best rides around, the tall ones, not the little scrummers. He thought we could help his players get that little bit further.

'You can't be playing with a full load,' he said, his arm creeping around Maeve's waist after we'd been talking rubbish for nearly an hour.

'What?' she said to him, her face blank.

I winked and he nodded at me.

'Ask your friend there.' His fingers were crawling around her backside.

'Stop, would ya,' she said, pushing him off.

'Bet your friend wouldn't say that,' he said, staring at me.

I brushed the second of confusion from my mind. And I thought of those candy cigarettes.

'D'ya have a smoke?' I asked.

'Now, now, you young things shouldn't be smoking.' He wagged his finger at us.

We coughed and laughed as he lit up the John Player Blues dangling from our lips, his hands hovering around my chin. We nodded to another West Coast Cooler and I could feel my head spin and I thought if this were to kill me, I wouldn't feel too bad at all. Patsy wrote his number on a coaster each for us, so we could phone him in case we wanted to meet the team.

'It'll be great craic,' he said. 'They're good-looking fellas, great craic all-to-gether.'

I laughed at the way he said *altogether* like it was three words.

'We've got to go,' I said sliding off the bar stool.

'So soon?'

'Yaw, like, we've an *appointment* to keep,' Maeve said, her face like stone.

'Too bad, ladies, too bad.' Patsy picked at something in his teeth.

On the way home Maeve tore the paper into little shreds.

'Fucking oul fella,' she said. 'We're not going there again, I'm tellin' you. It's no fun anymore.'

'Yeah,' I shrugged. My fingers curled around the slip of

145

paper.

*

Dad's on the split shift from one to ten. My hands shake as I trace the numbers around, my finger hot and swollen in the round hole of the phone dial. I look at my feet. My *Lady Lucks* lead the way.

'Thanks so much for calling,' he says, all formal. 'Sure, I'll meet you at that hotel, of course. Yes, we can make it tonight if you want. We've got a lot of ground to cover.'

I light another cigarette and blow smoke into the mouthpiece.

'You're welcome,' I say, trying to sound like Elkie Brooks.

I leave a note saying I'm going out with Maeve. I get the bus into town and wait in the lobby. I watch him walking towards me, a pinstriped jacket and a swagger. He gives me a small present wrapped in turquoise paper: a plastic cigarette holder.

'Because you're a lovely little lady,' he says quietly as he hands it to me.

I lean forward and without really thinking kiss him full on the lips like Mam used to with Dad. I think of the Milk Tray ad and smile.

'Jaysus,' he says, red in the face, 'calm down. Let's get out of here.'

'Yeah,' I say, my head hot.

We walk to his newly cleaned car and he drives us around until it's nearly completely dark.

'Let's go somewhere romantic,' he says, smiling.

'Oh, yes.' I wonder where he'll bring me.

'My ears are popping,' I say putting my hands over them as he drives up the mountains.

'That's because we're going up high.' His voice is shaky.

'If only Mam could see me now.' I laugh.

'Your mam?' he quickly takes his hand off my thigh.

'She died,' I say in a loud voice, looking right at him, glad I wore Mam's turquoise wedges, wondering if my feet would always fit into them, if I'd grow any more or was this it.

146

He parks alongside a line of cars, switches off the lights. We're on a plateau. The lights of Dublin twinkle. I think of the flickering pink candles on the last birthday cake Mam made for me. They sat on chocolate icing that melted with the heat. I try counting them but can't remember whether there were seven or eight.

The seats go flat at the touch of a button. He passes me a silver hipflask with the initials PMcD engraved in twirly writing on the front.

'Whiskey,' he says, 'if you want.'

I take a long drink and cough. I laugh as the roughness of his hands slides up my thighs. I scream as I feel his weight and the pushing and the pain and hot breath. My legs kick.

'Stop kicking,' he barks.

I stop moving. I think I stop breathing.

'Scream some more,' he whispers.

And I do. And I do.

*

Patsy would bring little presents every time we met. Trinket boxes engraved with elephants, bracelets with charms of hearts. I'd comb his hair and massage his feet.

When I'd come home after my dates with Patsy, sometimes Dad would glare and look at his watch. Other times he'd smile and hold out his arms. I'd always look at his hands. They were smaller than Patsy's. But still they were rough from the ice burns he'd get at work.

'When are you going to let me meet the fella you're so in love with?' he'd often ask.

'Dad, I've told you. There's no *one* boy.'

He'd shake his head.

'In my day we just courted a girl and then – '

' – like I said,' I'd say, blowing a Hubba Bubba bubble, 'I've got lots of friends who happen to be boys, right?'

'You know not to be doing anything you shouldn't be,' he said, one evening, his face scarlet. 'We wouldn't want a baby… like what happened to that young one up the road.'

147

'Of course,' I said sweetly. I closed *Flowers in the Attic* and wondered if he'd guessed I had a *real* boyfriend.

'That's my best girl.' He smiled proudly, switching on the TV.

I picked up the remote, butterflies in my stomach. 'Hey, can I watch *Eastenders*?' I asked, knowing that he'd clear off and leave me to gaze longingly at Dirty Den who was far more handsome than Patsy.

*

I was sure I'd have a good time with the rugby boys. Mam used to say to be good at something you had to keep trying till you got it right. *Practice makes perfect* was her motto. The under 21s rugby team lined up outside Patsy McDermot's hotel room timing each other with stopwatches. Over the three nights there were two Johns, three Pats, four Seáns, a Richard, a Tom, a Shane, a David, a James and a Gareth. I wore a mask with glitter and sparkling jewels on it.

'It's like the masks from Italy,' Patsy explained. 'From Venice, so secret lovers wouldn't be discovered.' He raised his bushy eyebrows.

I turned it over in my hands. It felt light. I liked the sparkles.

'Just in case you know any of the boys,' Patsy said. 'You know, or they know you.'

He was anxious, I think, that I wouldn't wear it. He was worried that I wouldn't do it. I could hear them jostling in the corridors, laughter and bets on who would go the longest. When Mam's coffin was lowered into the ground I'd promised myself that once I started something I'd finish it. Mam never got to finish so many things and Patsy had already given me some money so I couldn't say no now.

He handed me the hipflask and slipped through the door of the adjoining family room.

The mask felt like a second skin.

Tom was first. He said he was sorry, he didn't know what to do. I laughed, the whiskey kicking in and said I didn't know either. I'd only ever done it once. He fumbled and I giggled and

148

a few minutes later he cleared his throat and thanked me.

After Tom I closed my eyes and told myself that *not* feeling anything was okay. I pretended Mam was telling me to go on, like she used to when I was running the egg and spoon race.

Go on, she'd say. *You can do it.*

*

I'd always stay with Patsy longer to show him that he really was the special one. One evening he ordered room service. I asked for a Black Russian and chocolate ice-cream with strawberry sauce dribbled on top. I sat on the bed cross-legged in my black satin outfit and my *Lady Luck* heels. I hadn't worn Mam's turquoise wedges since our first time in the car. I was giddy and tired all at once.

I'd had a row with Dad who'd caught me smoking.

'I'm not going to let you go like her,' he'd shouted. 'You've to be home by nine even at weekends until you give that crap up.'

I'd nodded and not been able to sleep afterwards.

'Those boys play better on the field when they've been with you, Ita,' Patsy said. 'I just don't know how you do it.'

Despite having all the ice-cream we wanted at home – Dad still brought it home from work – I really enjoyed that ice-cream. Patsy sat in a wicker chair in the corner, watching me licking the spoon and moaned.

'I love you Patsy,' I said, my head light.

'You've brought happiness back into my life.'

'I can't stay long,' I whispered, thinking he wouldn't hear and maybe I could tiptoe out.

'What?' his eyes were half-closed, his tone sharp.

'I've to be back by nine.'

He opened his eyes. 'Lick that spoon, Ita.'

I licked, wanting to bite, to split the spoon with my teeth and feel that taste of blood, of metal. And I watched him, his eyes closed again, his hand jerking beneath his trousers, and wondered what he was thinking, wondered if he had a wife somewhere, asleep in a big, clean bed.

The last year of school put an end to our gallivanting, as Mrs Flynn put it. It was exam time and she wouldn't let Maeve out. Maeve didn't get what I saw in Patsy anyway, so she was thick with me. But I still thought of her as my friend. Now, though, being with Patsy was boring. He'd started telling me how his wife didn't understand him like I did. I didn't give a fuck about his life, his family.

A few weeks later I let Dad answer the telephone to Patsy. I sat on the top stair, giving myself carpet burn as I heard him curse. He told Patsy to fuck off and never to ring the house again or he'd call the police. And when I couldn't stop crying that night Dad even gave me half a Guinness with our pepperoni pizza. And he promised to bring home some *Vienetta* from work the next day.

His hand rested on my shoulder. 'Ita, you've to stay in. Do some proper study. You don't want to be letting your Mam down.'

I hugged him hard, the wetness of my tears on his jumper touching my cheek.

*

School was finished and Maeve was in London, training to be a famous actress in RADA. The lucky duck. I went to hairdressing school; I didn't get even half the points needed for college. I lasted three weeks. The skin on my hands cracked with the chemicals. All the girls had fellas and I hated them. And they hated me.

I quit.

The welfare money meant I could give Dad a bit of cash for the shopping. My beloved *Lady Lucks* finally wore their path to the black bin and I concluded that they'd just pushed me too far.

I'd discovered that I enjoyed reading and had bought loads of books at Mother Redcaps Market – a bag of them – and I'd the bag in my hand when I tried on *Size 38* with *Hecho en España* and *Piel* written on the soft leather lining in gold. They felt so light and wonderful I knew they were just right.

Funnily, it was on that same day I'd given in to Patsy's pleadings and agreed to meet. But it turned out that he just wanted to tell me one of the boys was getting married and that – *even* if I wanted to – those *get-to-gethers* could never happen again. I slapped him across the face hard, delighted I hadn't bothered dressing up, thrilled that I was just in jeans and a black top.

'You must be thick. Didn't my dad tell you to fuck off?' I sneered, feeling elated.

He looked odd without his usual hat. 'I didn't realise *you* wanted me to fuck off.'

'Maeve was right all along,' I said, imagining her singing on a stage. 'You're just an oul fella.'

'I'll be off, so,' he replied, sniffing.

As I watched him stand up, I could have sworn a tear lingered.

*

Later, when I got a job as a waitress in a café near the Powerscourt Shopping Centre, Dad was delighted. I tethered on my new heels, stuffing five quid tips down my cleavage. It was wearing them that I first met Matt, an archivist with long piano fingers and soft hands. I'd served him a large black coffee and he'd smiled. I wrote my number on a wine napkin and he called that very night.

We went to the cinema that weekend and we walked in the park, fingers curled around fingers, arms swinging. He told me he preserved things so that people could learn about the past. It was a shame, I said, that there weren't archivists in clothes; not like military uniforms or anything but normal people's clothes. He shrugged.

Sex was never mentioned. When he kissed me, it was on the cheek. I watched him drinking tea, the way his lip curled in satisfaction when he finished. I wondered what he'd be like in bed. I invited him home to meet Dad. He threw his arms around me, but the day he was due to come he rang me at the café.

'I'm not well,' he said. 'I'm not even at work.'

I counted to ten in my head.

His voice crackled. 'I'll make it up, Ita, I promise.'

I fell asleep on the sofa that night, tears streaking my face, the sound of Dad threatening to beat the bastard who'd broken my heart.

*

He made amends, though, with a surprise holiday to the Canary Islands. Work and Dad were in on the surprise and Dad laughed, saying he'd already started on his father-of-the-bride speech and that this one was a keeper, after all.

My *Size 38s* nearly killed me on the flight, the straps tight around my ankles. We giggled like children as Matt massaged my feet in the hotel. We drank 7-Up and my *Size 38s* only came off when we swam in the pool. He insisted I wear them to bed and he licked the soles before slowly kissing me all over. It was the first time we'd slept together. It felt fun, lovely, new. We kissed.

One night he covered my eyes with his hands as we made love. His body heavy on me, he pushed hard.

I screamed, 'No!'

He rolled off me. 'Fuck it, Ita, you're the one who was dying to… and now – '

' – it's not you,' I sobbed, sweating.

He put the pillow over his head. 'Oh just forget it,' he shouted. 'Just go to sleep.'

But, instead of sleeping, I pulled a cardi around my pink nighty and went for a walk in my yellow flipflops. There was a light breeze and revellers were partying in beautiful dresses, heels, freshly pressed shirts. I smiled; remembering Mam putting on her face. There was nothing about these transformations that excited me any more. I couldn't tell whether it was the gentle click-clack over cobblestoned streets or the glamour that made Matt love heels so much. I sat on the sand watching the lovers and beach parties in the distance and cried as I rubbed the grains of sand up and down my legs.

'Sorry,' Matt said as we walked along the beach the next morning, hand in hand. 'I thought you were game.'

I closed my eyes and breathed the sea air into my lungs. *Game*, I repeated in my head. *Game.*

We saw a cargo of bananas come to dock. I stood, transfixed at the ladies, all smiles and full mouths singing, and the men, hauling orange crates onto land. Something reminded me of a book I'd read by Jean Rhys. *Wide Sargasso Sea.* I gazed at the women's hips as they swayed in tune with their songs.

'Let's go.' Matt pulled at me. 'They're just bloody bananas.'

I knew, then, he wasn't a keeper. As my mind captured the image of the woman with the mustard yellow skirt and peacock blue blouse, I realised that I was well on that slope to being the madwoman in the attic.

*

It wasn't the thoughts of that book that saved me, though.

I bumped into one of Patsy's boys in The Foggy Dew. It was noisy and smoky but I knew that nape of a neck. I stared at Tom until he looked. His face darkened. He quickly turned away. Ha, I thought, you were happy to have your fun with me until you found a real girlfriend.

'Hey,' I called after him.

He glanced back again. I thought he shook his head but I couldn't be sure.

'Motherfucker,' I shouted and blew smoke after him, wishing him ill, wishing him a horrible death.

I watched him leave. A girl, neat like a paperclip, trotting behind him, anxiously looked at me as I flicked ash in their direction.

'And fuck you too,' I shouted.

*

I have a recurring nightmare about shopping with Mam and getting stuck in the changing room. And smoke snakes around her neck, strangling her, and I'm reaching out as she fades, fades, fades.

Last night I woke in a cold sweat. I remembered clearly how the ladies in the Canaries moved in their bare feet, more graceful than any ballerina, more beautiful than a pop star in heels.

When I was a waitress, I believed secretaries knew *things*. Now, as a secretary in a law firm, I await instructions, knowledge in my silence.

Every evening, Dad and I sit on the sofa with our slippers; he with his paper, me with my novel both half-reading, half-watching the flickering image on the TV. We sneak happy smiles at each other.

One night, after Dad went to bed I stuffed my high-heeled shoes in a black bag. I put a little kiss for luck on them. And then I smoked my last cigarette.

*

That was a year ago.

I am dressed in a smart yellow dress. I vomit my carrot and coriander soup onto purple pansies two doors up from the office.

Someone taps me on the shoulder.

'You okay?'

I wipe my mouth, take a deep breath and stand straight. 'Clearly not.'

He's wearing ridiculously white runners and a dark grey suit. His eyes are bright. 'I work in the same office as you,' he ventures, his eyes darting across my face. 'I'm one of the trainees. Starting a new career. Dave's the name.'

I'm searching in vain for a glimpse of memory that holds something of Dave.

'I needed to use the fax machine. I'm such a dunce,' he says, blushing. 'And you helped me.'

'Oh,' I reply, rotating my left ankle.

'Come for a coffee,' he suggests, 'when you're feeling better.'

He scuffs his runner on the pavement.

'How about now?'

'Right now?'

I nod.

We walk back to the office, the silence between us peppered with his shy glances.

He looks at my feet.

'You used to wear heels.'

'Decided to give my feet a break. Although... ' I pause, watching his full lips move into a smile, my tummy fuzzy. 'My back is killing me. Did you know when your back gets used to counterbalancing or whatever the hell it has to do to help you walk in three-inch-heels – that when it doesn't have to compensate, you know... it just doesn't know what to be doing.'

'You're mad,' he says, laughing.

Maybe I am.

And I smile broadly, not caring about my yellow teeth.

Roma

A necklace is fingered: a ring turned.
All things have possibility: everything has movement.

*

Mary stood by the old oak kitchen table at which her son sat over breakfast. She remembered the feel of the lacquered table where she'd sat across from Sepp in a tiny café in Bamberg, Germany. Sepp had leaned over, an unhinged twinkle in his eye, and announced to her, a complete stranger, that she was *full of things*. He was referring to her collection of rings and the several silver necklaces that sat on her neck as if they were part of her. In a moment of madness, she'd slid her hand across the sheen of the table until the tips of her fingers touched the tips of his. The rush of love in her red cheeks and light laugh. That day, the day that set the rest of her life in motion, was almost thirty years ago.

It was a Saturday morning in late February now and Sepp was seven years in an Irish grave. She wrapped her hands around the large Stephen Pearce mug of coffee and sighed.

'I've been to the doctor's again,' she finally said, 'a specialist.'

'Oh,' her son said flatly.

She watched his face closely. He was like his father. It was rare that his face would express his direct thoughts. She often imagined how life would have been had his twin, a girl, survived. She had waited for and received her boy. If she had felt the baby was a girl, would her daughter have lived and her son died? She'd bled a little and they had told her to rest. She was too big. They told her not to worry. To keep her feet up. Pregnancy was a gift, a miracle. She should have been grateful for any sign of life, not given preference to a son or daughter. But she had. Deep within her she had wanted a son more than anything. She had what she desired.

'Well,' she chirped, 'it's a bit of good and bad news.'

Dirk placed a piece of bitten toast on a plate. She could see a hint of alarm in his eyes. As she spoke she felt she had stepped outside of herself.

'My time has come. I don't want to end up like Sheila with her arthritis as well as dementia in a nursing home. My choice, I said to the doctor.'

There was a momentary pause before he replied.

'What? What are you talking about? You're... too young.'

Dirk stuffed half a slice of toast into his mouth.

She moved closer, put her arm around him, aware of her voice becoming more high-pitched. 'I've been diagnosed with the big C.'

He took a loud slurp of coffee and swallowed the toast.

'I'm fifty-five. It can happen to anyone. Breast cancer. Though it's quite advanced, I said to the doctor that nature should take its own course to which he quite agreed. Really, there's no point me going through all the pain of radiotherapy and whatnot. Just think back to your father. In intensive care for days and for what? At the end of the day there's nothing you can do to escape your fate.'

Mary thought of the café again. She remembered not ever considering consequences; fear was not part of her vocabulary then. Now she could see the fear of loss filter through Dirk. As a child he used to announce, like a faulty Christ *I am the son of Mary and Jo.* He could never get comfortable with either abbreviation for Josef and would switch between Sepp and Jo. It was as if he knew his father wouldn't be with him for long. Mary flipped her lilac pump on and off her foot. Life was there and then it was not.

'But treatment will prolong your life, even cure you. You can't just say no. And,' Dirk looked at her exasperated, 'don't tell me the doctor agreed. I really don't think he can do that, professionally.'

Mary fixed her shoe back on her foot. She laughed, feeling calm again. 'He agreed on a personal note. It's a series of choices: give in to medicine, give up on life or fight on all

157

fronts. Of course he did ask that I consult my family and I told him that my son would do what's best for his mother.'

'Is it really just about your choice?' He stood up, challenging.

'Tell me you *don't* have days when you wish you could throw in the towel. To just not bother.'

For a moment, she couldn't look at him. Really, what was she thinking? It was almost two years after he'd attempted suicide. Who *was* she kidding about choices?

'This is different.'

'Why? Maybe it's my body saying it's had enough.'

'But you're making the decision not to cure your body. You're… '

He looked like he was about to cry.

'What? I'm what? There is no cure.' She took a step away from him as they stood facing each other, her hand resting on the kitchen table. 'You think I'm backing down, slinking into a corner like some old cat wanting to die. I can tell by that reprimanding look on your face. I always thought you would have made a good teacher. Always on the lookout for something to correct.'

'I didn't say that. I meant – '

'No, *Dietrich*, you didn't. But know this about me. I am not the one giving up.'

Dirk sniffed, looked away. 'Is this the death you had hoped for?'

Mary coughed, feeling dizzy. 'Give your old mother a hug for goodness sake.' She paused. 'And don't be asking me those sort of questions.'

'Sorry.' He spoke quietly.

'You know, sometimes when we suffer the most we can't even acknowledge it to ourselves.'

*

Dirk was taking her to Rome, one of the few European cities she hadn't been to with Sheila. This she discovered by (mistakenly) opening the envelope which contained their tickets and hotel vouchers. He'd booked an expensive hotel right in the tourist area of central Rome, arranged time off with work and ensured their passports were up to date. She wanted to reprimand him. Instead, she apologised for spoiling her surprise and allowed him to help pack her clothes. He made sure she'd plenty of layers in the form of several cardigans; she'd been feeling the cold, any hint of cold, lately. The trip, she felt, put the matter of time into a different perspective. Suddenly there was something to enjoy, not something that was lingering on the horizon. He couldn't have done a more wonderful thing.

*

On the plane, they ate their breakfast, stealing glances and sneaking shy smiles at each other and out the window, like young honeymooners. At the airport, with everything gleaming and clean, they bought their tickets to Roma Termini Station and boarded the Leonardo Express. Dirk took to giggling, pointing out the window, showing Mary the different styles of houses, fields and villages leading into central Rome. The wind blew right into their faces, biting, as they stepped off the train.

Mary tried to fix her hair back in place.

'We'll have to get you an Italian silk scarf,' said Dirk.

'What, and make me look like a housewife?'

She would not turn into Sheila with headscarves of peaches, even if Dirk did mean well. He pulled the two cases behind him in silence.

She looked around. 'It's like a shopping centre in here with the windows and the stalls.'

'Come on,' Dirk said, stopping and taking hold of the cases by the pull-grips again. 'Let's get to the hotel and check in.'

'There was really no need to do this.'

'That's why I did it. Because you hadn't asked for it.'

'I just want to say... ' Mary thought strangely that she was like a child asking for sweets. 'In case I forget or don't get a chance, but I just want to say thank you. I mean that. It's one of the most wonderful things anyone has ever done for me. I don't know... ' She could feel her face redden whether from cold sweat or embarrassment she could no longer tell. 'Dirk,' she said, turning to face him, 'it's perfect.'

*

'*Buongiorno Signore e Signora. Dove andate?*'

Mary looked to Dirk who held out the leaflet about the hotel. 'Hotel La Notte,' he said, with what Mary thought sounded like a decent Italian accent.

'A very popular hotel.'

'Oh, so you speak English,' Mary said.

'Of course. Many tourists in Rome, *Signora*. But I speak better Italian and the ladies like the Italian.'

Mary laughed.

'My daughter is studying English at Rome University,' the driver continued, glancing casually in the rear-view mirror as the traffic weaved in and out of lanes, the chorus of tooting horns almost melodic. 'She speaks English very good but it is good for me to try and improve so that I can speak with her at dinner.'

'Really, well that's very good,' Mary said, leaning forward in her seat, grabbing the back of the front passenger seat for support. 'Dirk did a short course in Italian. Dirk, my son,' she said pointing to him. She nudged Dirk who rolled his eyes and looked out the window. 'But of course he's too shy to use it,' she added.

'Where are you from?'

'We are from Dublin, Ireland,' Mary said, emphasising the 'ire' bit of Ireland.

'I see the bombs have stopped,' he said, looking in the mirror, trying to catch her eye. 'I see the IRA and the other side… What are they called?'

'UVF, UDA, there are lots of others that see themselves on the other side.' Dirk didn't hide his irritation.

'So, it is a safe place now?'

'We haven't had a bomb in Dublin since 1974,' said Dirk.

Mary felt somewhat embarrassed by Dirk's need to spout his idea of truth at every opportunity. This trip would open his eyes, she thought as she yawned. 'You must visit,' she

160

encouraged the driver.

'We're crossing Piazza di Spagna now.' He hurtled across the piazza, taking Via del Babuino followed by two swift sharp rights onto Via Margutta. 'Your hotel,' he said as he drove up what seemed to be impossibly narrow streets. 'And where you are staying is very good for the sightseeing. And of course the shopping for the lady. You have Rome's most famous shopping street Via dei Condotti just here!'

'*Grazie.*' Here she was, a woman of her age, frolicking in Rome. '*Roma*,' she exclaimed. 'I can't believe we are actually here!'

'Nor can I,' Dirk said, grinning as he pocketed the last of the change after leaving a generous tip.

The hotel was housed in a former seminary but had a modern twist with bright colours, lots of plastic, wood and leather furniture and contemporary pebbled floors. They paused to admire the vaulted frescoed ceiling which overlooked a marble altar and cathedral-like stained-glass windows. It was like walking into an Andy Warhol picture in the middle of a chapel.

'You'd never know this was a former chapel, would you?' Dirk said.

'Not in a million years. Well I hope the rooms are as nice as this.'

Dirk wheeled the cases up to the reception desk. Letting them rest with a bang on the polished floor, he handed his passport and the booking documents to the perfectly tanned, groomed man behind the counter.

'You are in rooms 305 and 306 so you can take the elevator up to the third floor. That is the orange floor. Enjoy your stay here.' The man smiled stiffly.

'You know, Dirk, we should have done this long ago, you and I. We should have gone away after your father died. I should have dragged you somewhere, got you out in the real world.'

Dirk smiled. They stepped out of the lift in silence and walked along the corridor looking at the strip of floor that lit up orange as they walked on it. The ceilings were white and the walls were orange.

'Oh, let's see my room first,' Mary said, making a beeline for her door. She decided that this trip was about cramming as much into a short space of time as was humanly possible, enjoying as a child would, abandoning oneself to the moment. The walls were cream with furniture of polished dark wood. A scent of jasmine came off several cream candles either side of the large vase of flowers.

'I have lots of bright yellow daisy-like flowers. Just like lots of suns in my room.'

She laughed and suddenly, she didn't care as she looked at Dirk, growing into his father, now witnessing her joyous and happy as if she were a child. Everyone, she thought, deserves a second chance.

*

That evening they stopped in Piazza Navona to admire the fountain and soak up a bit of the atmosphere. It seemed Rome was the city of eternal fountains. Majestic buildings, not unlike the government buildings back in Dublin, lined the piazza which was long and quite narrow.

'I don't know why I thought all piazzas were squares,' Dirk said to Mary, 'but it's sort of disappointing.'

Mary laughed. 'Just listen to yourself.'

'I know… '

'It's just silly. I mean look at it,' she said, her arms outstretched. 'You've got the fountain of four rivers by Bernini right in front of you; a real, live piece of art, and look at all these people creating more art. It's like the buskers on Grafton Street but with a bit more style, you know, mixed in with the fashionable Romans out for their stroll before their dinner. Come on, lighten up, we're in Rome, for God's sake!'

He started humming the tune by Perez Prado from the Guinness advert. 'Da-da-da-da-da – '

'You know the advert is called *Anticipation*,' Mary said.

A man with a black top hat was listening to their conversation. The rest of his clothes were modern but it was the top hat and what he was holding in his hands, a large pack of cards, that caught Mary's attention. The man saw her looking.

'You like the magic?' he said, standing up from his adopted resting place, the black metal fence which protected the fountain.

Mary smiled.

He stroked his long, thin beard. 'I can tell that you like the magic,' he said moving closer, a smile curling on his lips.

'I am magic,' said Mary, flushing.

The man laughed. 'Please, *Signora*, let me introduce myself. I am Pedro, the best magician in all of Spain. I am travelling all of Europe, bringing my magic with me to ladies like you.'

'Thank you, Pedro, but we have a dinner appointment.'

Mary looked through Dirk. 'We're not in any hurry. Let Pedro show me his magic.' She laughed, offering her hand to him. 'I am Mary and this is Dirk. We are from Ireland.'

'Very pleased to meet you. The Irish ladies are the finest in the world,' he bowed, taking Mary's hand and brushing his lips against it. 'And what a powerful stone you have in that ring you're wearing.'

Mary turned her amethyst ring on her finger. It was the first piece of jewellery Sepp had bought her.

Amongst the dark hair, Pedro had perfect streaks of grey, captive in black dye. He was older than he looked.

'Pick one,' Pedro said, holding his cards out. 'Just ask your own self what you want to know.'

'Go on,' Mary said.

Dirk picked one and held it tightly.

'Look at the card.' Pedro nodded in encouragement.

Dirk looked at the card and frowned. 'What cards are these?'

'These are inner child cards. When you pick a card your spirit is telling you something. Show me the card.'

Dirk held it up.

'Aha. Your spirit has picked The Wizard. A spiritual teacher is near. You must open yourself out and build a bridge between the child that is inside of you and the man that you are. But remember,' he pointed his index finger towards the sky, 'let yourself be inspired and you find the way of the bull, the Taurus.'

He turned to Mary, smiling. 'And now to you, my dear lady. Ask your spirit what it wants to tell you.'

'I already know,' she said, shaking her head.

'There are always extra messages that we don't hear. Pick a card.'

Mary reached out. 'I've got people skipping on mine,' she said, disappointed.

'The Three of Crystals. Now that's interesting. It's about community spirit and cooperation yet each person has his own path in the society. Look at the rope in the card.'

Mary and Dirk leaned over.

'It's a rainbow,' Dirk said, taking Mary's hand and patting it. 'So there is hope.'

'A bridge,' Pedro said, making the shape of a bridge with his hands.

'Another bridge? We want magic!' Mary shook her head.

'But bridges are hope. You need to play and enjoy. That, and nothing else, is what living is really about.'

Pedro removed his top hat and with it his wig, revealing a shiny bald head.

'Things are not always as they seem.' He raised his eyebrows. 'I will leave you now, dear travellers. I bid you a *buona sera*.'

And with that he placed his hair and hat back on his head, snapped his cards shut and was swallowed up into the throng of strollers, tourists and entertainers.

Dirk and Mary looked at each other. Dirk shook his head, bewildered. 'It's weird. I thought he was a trickster or something, you know, I didn't trust him, but a few things he said rang true so strongly that it set the hair on the back of my neck on end.'

'But he was a trickster. I read somewhere once that people come and go in your life. That some come for a reason, some for a season, and some to stay. Pedro is not the latter two so he must have come for a reason.'

They approached the Trevi fountain from Via del Corso. The street vendors with posters of *La Dolce Vita* for sale were the first hint Mary noticed that they were near finding this flashy, sparkling, monumental jewel. The second hint was the sound of running water above the hubbub of shoppers darting from chainstores to tiny boutiques filled with leather gloves in every colour imaginable. When they reached the fountain they looked at it in silence amid the flashes of cameras, cries of wonder of countless tourists, and the inhalations of the cigar-puffing local Romeos. Mary threw a coin in. She felt tearful, suddenly, watching her reflection reappear.

'Shall we meander to our place of dining, my dear lady?' Dirk asked her, a giggle escaping from his lips.

'Yes, my dear Oscar Wilde, yes we will.'

There were times, she thought, when he got it just right. They walked arm-in-arm, zigzagging between the wanderers and wonderers, ducking to avoid other people's photos, before taking the left exit down yet another narrow street back towards Piazza Navona.

'I feel I've been here before, like I know something in these streets,' Mary said, still linking Dirk's arm.

'I love it so far,' he said, his eyes following the wiggles of yet another set of *belle ragazze* out for an evening stroll before their dinner. 'I wouldn't say no to living here, in fact.'

'You know,' she said, letting go of his arm in an oddly theatrical gesture, 'I now believe we should never have left Germany. Ireland will be the making of you but it was his breaking. Sepp's, I mean. Had we stayed maybe you'd both be stronger in your own ways.' She started walking again, her pace quickening, not wanting to look at Dirk.

'Ireland isn't necessarily the making of me, you know.'

'Why do you stay, then?'

'I like what I'm doing.'

'I always thought you wasted your talent. All that reading to end up in a library. Even if you can call yourself a professional.'

'Where better a place to continue reading?' Dirk laughed uneasily.

Mary knew she should stop, knew she should remember that less than an hour ago they had become enthralled in the magic that a bald man was weaving.

'Yes, but didn't you ever want to do more than handing out books to other people to read? What's that, a bit better than stock control in a tiny library? Come on.'

Dirk spoke quietly. 'Maybe. I just didn't want what I was made for. And I've been fighting it all this time.'

'Maybe. Maybe not.' She stopped walking as they crossed the road and went back into the oblong Piazza. 'And this giggling business... ' Her voice trailed off.

They crossed the road in silence and stood, looking at yet more sculptures, crowded cafes, the hum of chitchat and the squeals of laughter.

'I know you're suffering, Mother, but – '

'Since when did you address me as Mother? Why are you doing it now, Dirk – why now?' Mary turned to him, her eyes filled with tears. 'You don't remember of course, but I tried and tried to get you to call me Mammy or Mama or something that resembled Mother when you were little but you insisted on copying your father in the way you addressed me.'

'Really?' Dirk frowned.

'Yes, *really.*'

'I always thought... I mean I can't remember you trying... ' Dirk paused. 'I mean, of course I don't remember you trying, I was too young, but I always thought you wanted to be called Mary.'

'But in having you that's what I became. Your mother. At least when I think of you I know that you'll always be the son of Mary Horn.' She felt nauseous. All of this would soon change. But she shouldn't think of those things. 'Come on, let's just get dinner now, shall we?'

They were dining in Taverna Parione. It was a restaurant that had come recommended from a friend who knew someone who had lived in Rome, studying in the Georgian University for a few years. It was a favourite haunt because of the generous portions and good value. It was not your typical tourist restaurant, they both realised as they walked in to the buzz of Italian chatter. There was not a tourist in sight. It was full of locals after a hard day's shopping.

'This is wonderful,' Mary exclaimed, handing her coat to the waiter. 'Oh, let's get a bottle of nice wine.'

They sat and opened the menus. There was no sign of anyone speaking English and translating the menu. It would be hit and miss.

Dirk flicked his hair. The last time they had been out in a public place for an evening dinner was after Sepp's funeral and he'd hardly spoken to her. He'd been cornered – or allowed himself to remain so – by the German relatives. He'd loved every minute of it: the conversations and catching-ups let him forget why he was there. Now, she thought, she would have him to herself. The boy whose curls she used to stroke. The baby for whom she took up knitting. The only baby. The one that just kept on living.

'Oh, it's an adventure,' he said, suddenly touching her hand. 'Let's see what pick and mix we get!'

'I think they do that here, you know – have pasta to start but in smaller portions. Go on to the toilets and spy on the tables as you walk past them so you can let me know what others are eating.'

'Let's just try the menu ourselves.'

'Dirk.' She could hear the sharpness. She sighed. She was right. She was always going to be the mother.

'Alright then,' he sighed as he got up, left the table.

Mary twisted her hair around her index finger and looked around at the other tables. There were all sorts and shapes of bowls, plates, baskets filled with bread, pasta, salads, hams, and cheeses. Wine and water flowing amid the buzz of excited chat and the clatter of dishes and roars of stressed chefs. People living. There were small tables of couples, friends, and larger ones of what looked like people straight from work, some looking bored, some, already having had a little bit too much to drink, being over-animated at the table – or maybe that was the Italian way? She smiled as the waiter laid down a basket of bread. She picked up the menu and pointed to a ham dish and a selection of cheese. '*Per favore*,' she said, imagining she had come here and not Bamberg at twenty-two. She tried her best to pronounce some of the main courses. The waiter smiled. It was all part of it, she thought.

The waiter brought wine, water, cheese, ham and bread.

Mary smiled widely, tried the wine and nodded her appreciation. She looked around and thought to herself how moments like these seemed to come from nowhere; and yet many more before them had to have happened for these few, right now. She took a sip of wine.

Dirk approached the table.

'So they brought bread? And ham and cheese? And wine? And water? Wow!'

'No.' She smiled smugly.

He laughed. 'You're one dark horse sending me on a wild goose chase like that.'

'No, Dirk, I just chanced my arm and ordered. I got through it and hey presto, like Pedro this evening, we have our food.'

'You must have had to do that when you went to Germany first,' he said, rolling Parma ham onto some bread and popping it in his mouth. It seemed to melt on his tongue. 'This food is *good*.'

'We are in Roma, darling,' she said, 'where the wine is like water. So, Germany. What do you want to know?'

'Everything. Why you went, who you went with, where you went, how Sepp came into it. Spill the beans.' Dirk took a drink of wine.

'Well,' Mary polished off the last bit of cheese dipped in honey. She licked her lips. 'Well, to start with, I was around your age when I went over. I'd finished college and wanted to live a little – you know, explore, get out and about.'

'I can imagine.'

'Actually, you can't imagine. Because you've never felt that way because we never held you back. And you've never needed to explore the world. But you know what? That's okay. That's just who you are. And that's who I was… at the time.'

'I have,' he said, cleaning his mouth.

Mary nodded at the waiter. '*Sì*,' she said, grinning as he topped up their wine.

'I have felt that way. I just didn't know what to do with those feelings.'

'You could have said something instead of taking tablets.'

168

She drained her glass in one, filled it up again.

She watched him control himself so that he would appear not to react. He looked away momentarily.

'Weren't we talking about Germany?'

'I've ordered veal for you and lamb for me for mains. I skipped the pasta if that's okay.'

'Fine. So. You were the same age as me. Why Germany?'

'Because I studied German. Why else? It's not as if I'd pick a country off the map for the sake of it. So, I'd left college with a degree in English and German and off I headed to Berlin. *That* didn't last long.'

'Why not?'

'Suffice it to say I met a few people that I didn't get on with so I moved on. Headed south. Frankfurt. It appealed because– ' She laughed loudly. 'Because, believe it or not,' she shook her head. 'It's such a silly reason but seemed logical then. Because Heidi had gone to Frankfurt and survived so I reckoned I could too.'

Dirk looked at her. 'Heidi? As in the books?'

She laughed. 'Oh, here comes our food.'

'Wow, this is Italy alright,' Dirk said. 'Mind the plate – it'll burn the fingers off you.'

'Enjoy.' The waiter bowed.

'I loved Heidi when I was little. She was my idol and you cling to the things you know, the scent of familiarity.'

'But didn't you meet in Berlin?'

'No, sure he'd never lived in Berlin. We met in – '

'But… ' Dirk put his cutlery down on the table. He'd started into cubed potatoes and a heavy-looking mushroom sauce with the veal.

Mary sighed. 'Hmm. How is your veal?'

'But you used to bring me to visit them. In Berlin. Yes, it's good.'

'Look, we went out of courtesy to his family. That was all. Your father grew up in Frankfurt and his family moved to Berlin after the wall came down.'

'And that's it?'

'That's it.'

'His own mother had to watch him being buried.'

'But you know,' Mary said, 'Frankfurt was a very conservative city and I was running out of money and needed to get a job to avoid going home. So fate took me to Bamberg. Bamberg and Sepp.'

Dirk's eyes lit up. 'And me.'

'Not quite you, yet, Dirk. I got a job teaching English at the University of Bamberg. One of the best years of my life. Sepp... swept me off my feet.' She laughed and, leaning over the table, ruffled his hair. She sat back and took a drink. She waved her empty glass around.

Dirk signalled to the waiter to bring another bottle.

'Not only did he sweep me off my feet, I got pregnant with twins.'

She watched Dirk pick up the crumbs from the tablecloth with his forefinger, lick it, and collect more crumbs.

He stopped, looked at her.

'Twins?'

She smiled, took a drink of wine. 'Sepp told you, didn't he? I always told him I just couldn't bear to talk about it. They took her away. I never saw her.'

'I had a twin?'

'So he didn't tell you.'

Dirk shook his head. He slowly drank some wine. He looked at the couple at the table beside them.

'I bet they're honest with each other. They have that look on their faces. Like they have nothing to hide.'

'Everybody hides something, Dirk. Don't be so naive. Oh, and you'll have to thank that friend of yours for the recommendation. I bet we won't get nicer food than tonight.'

'It's a cousin of a friend of Angela's.'

She watched him closely. He was holding back tears. He was being who she wanted him to be.

'Why didn't you have any more children?'

Mary wiped the corners of her mouth with her napkin and cleared her throat. 'Fate.'

'Fate's a cop-out.'

'The doctor said I was too old and Jo was too stressed. Who

were we to question authority?'

'Didn't you question everything else? Weren't you the rebels of your time?' Dirk took a long drink of wine.

'No, we didn't.' She paused. 'Tell me, how's Angela these days?'

'Forget Angela. I want to know about my twin. The other children.'

'The ones that never lived. Ha! There were no others. It was you and only you.'

Dirk shook his head. 'Jesus, I don't know what to believe, you know?'

And Mary shrugged, an uneasy feeling in the pit of her stomach alongside a buzz in her head. She laughed loudly and then concentrated on her words as she spoke slowly.

'It's always been you, Dirk, my only boy.'

She reached across the table.

Dirk withdrew his hands, bit his thumbnail before speaking. 'Angela and I don't see as much of each other as we used to, since – '

' – you'd probably be living together or engaged by now had you not told her.'

He took a drink of wine, shaking the bottle, the last drops plopping into his glass. 'More hiding and brushing under the carpet. I didn't want *not* to tell her. I thought she'd understand. She was convinced that she had something to do with it.' He paused. 'A bit like my twin, I'm thinking. I just kicked her till she gave up. Without ever realising it.'

Mary drummed her fingers on the table. 'There was something in Angela's eyes that matched yours.'

The waiter hovered around them. 'The delicious desserts?' he suggested.

Mary shook her head, waved him away.

'Maybe that's why she wasn't for me.'

'There's someone for everyone, don't you know, but you can't wait for them to appear. Not that you're going to be every girl's fancy, but you have to be open to it. You've had your fun. Now it's time to think about really living. I mean you have a house and – '

'What are you talking about? I don't have a house.'

'You do. Sheila got Mammy's house, you get my house.'

Dirk shook his head. 'No. It's not my house. I don't intend to bring some wife back when you die and – '

'When I die.'

'When you die and – '

Mary clapped her hands. 'Right. Resolution time. I'm proposing that we ban talking about anything to do with death, dying, attempted death or the possibility of dying.'

Dirk looked towards the couple at the other table. 'Fine.'

'My Oskie,' she whispered to the air, 'I'm so sorry.'

*

They were doing a walking tour of Rome for St Patrick's Day. They nabbed one of their fellow walkers to take a photograph of them. They stood, holding hands, surrounded by the mass and power of St Peter's Square. Mary was squinting slightly in the sun and Dirk had a grin on his face. Mary wondered why they had picked St Peter's Square for the photograph; surely there had been more intimate and endearing places? A seat at the Coliseum, the Trevi Fountain, a corner of the Pantheon?

'I want to see myself standing, dying but still standing, amongst the memorials of the dead. Bring me to Pompeii before I die.'

'What the lady wants is what the lady gets,' Dirk said as he wrapped his arms around her.

Jack

The image of the coffin would not leave his mind. As he pushed open the front door, he paused momentarily, wishing the key would break in the lock so that he would not have to go into the house. So that he could go somewhere else, anywhere, any place other than what was now rightfully his – and nobody else's – home. He'd purposely left the heating on full blast so that it wouldn't be cold. He shivered. What *do* people do the day they become an orphan?

He went into the front room and looked around. The room hadn't been decorated since she'd done it up after his father had died. His teenage paintings of coffins, expressions of grief still remained on the wall. He stood up, took one of them down, and stomped on the glass with his highly polished black shoe.

'Fuck you!' he shouted at the glass as it broke in five clean breaks. And then he laughed.

Who did he belong to now? Auntie Sheila still hovered, in her moments of lucidity, trying to be the do-gooder she always was. She was living in a care home now, dementia having finally driven her from the only home she had known. He knew she'd left the money from the house sale in her will to him.

'Well there's nothing you can do now, Sheila,' he'd said at the funeral, wishing that she had died instead of Mary. 'But you know,' he'd added, feeling slightly guilty as he looked at her, sure she recognised him, sure she knew he was himself and not Sepp, his dead father. 'I know Mary would've been glad we had each other. You were such a rock for her when Sepp died.'

Tears rolled down Sheila's cheeks. 'You poor, poor boy. You are all alone now,' she'd said, her peach and cream headscarf fluttering in the wind.

He remembered how, when Sepp died, Sheila had come over and cooked for a few days – or was it weeks?

'She's tidying,' Sheila had said when Mary locked herself in the bedroom. 'The room needs tidying.'

Sheila would help him carry the tray upstairs and leave it outside her door. While Dirk had painted the coffins, compartmentalising everything into boxes, Mary had been tidying her mind, tying her feelings into nice bunches, so that she could present herself to the world.

He wished he had brothers or sisters now. What would they be doing? How would they be acting? They would be with him, probably, sorting through the house, organising the paperwork, getting probate arranged. There was so much to do, yet suddenly none of it seemed urgent or necessary. He sat back on the sofa. What could he compartmentalise now? Who would help him tidy the mess that death leaves? Dirk wanted to have nothing to do with the practicalities of death. He didn't want to have to register her death, inform the electrical and gas companies that she was dead and to put all bills in his name. Get the bank accounts and post office accounts changed over to his name. He had no idea how much money she had in the accounts, and the thoughts of finding out and spending that money, her hard-earned and long-saved money, made him feel nauseous.

He cleaned up the glass and burned the painting in the grate before drinking several whiskeys. He prowled around the house, touching the walls, drinking more whiskey before finally falling into bed at just past midnight.

He dreamed he was in an Oxfam shop and picked up an exceptionally beautiful photo album for sale.

'It is second hand,' the svelte, trendily-dressed red-haired shop assistant told him, 'but it is as good as new.'

And he purchased it immediately, not bothering to open it and look inside. It was the cover that attracted him. It had horizontal minute panels stuffed with something soft and covered in wine red velvet. It had a rich, luscious feel to it and Dirk imagined that he would use it to gather together old photographs of his parents. It would be special, his own memory bank. He walked home, noting how the sun shone brightly. He started planning the order of the photographs and calculating how long it would take him to complete the album.

About an hour or so, he reckoned, excluding labelling each page, for which purpose he bought a black felt tip pen. The walk home was short and he was glad that it didn't take him long to get home. He gathered his boxes of photos, placing them carefully on the kitchen table, ready to begin the work. It was now only a few hours after burying his mother and his eyes were as dry as a bone, his heart, having felt like lead most of the day was now light, almost relieved.

The previous day to this dream, after the removal of his mother from the funeral home to the church – she was one of three to be removed that October afternoon, a conveyor-belt of the dead – he had returned to the house and hunted, like a man possessed, for photographs. They were mainly kept in one of the drawers of the dresser, which no longer seemed so large. It stood in the same place in the kitchen, as it had done for as long as he could remember. It stood, mocking in its continued existence, and with a shiver as he opened the drawer and piled the envelopes and Kodak wallets full of photographs onto the kitchen table for sorting, he thought that the dresser would still be the same after he had passed away. There were hundreds of them, not in any order; sepia, black-and-white and colour photos of eras gone and present all mixed up, stuffed into whatever wallet had space to accommodate an extra photograph at the time. A numbness spread through him.

He looked at the pile, but not seeing what it was. He could feel a burning heat behind his eyes and his nostrils flared involuntarily as the tears sprung to his eyes. He did not want to cry, that was something he had told himself he would not do. He would not cry because he was really only crying for himself. She had passed away and was no longer suffering. That was what he had to concentrate on, *her* happiness and joy. But there was no guarantee that she was happy, or joyful, or even that she now knew what those words really meant, now that she had supposedly reached the other side, the side of clarity and reward, now that she was supposedly united with Jo. Would they greet each other in German as they bounded through the meadows of heaven, reunited at last? Dirk's nostrils flared again and, despite himself, he put his head in his hands and

175

wept like a child. He howled and wept, giving into the sorrow sweeping over him, enveloping him, covering him like a perversely kind ghost. Like an instinctive ghost who knew what was good for him.

In his dream, he opened the album, feeling the smooth touch of the velvet, his heart soaring. A sepia photograph of a mixed race family stared back at him. To the left was a tall, thin man, a smile etched across his face, a knowing face. Both hands rested on the narrow shoulders of a young teenage girl, dressed in an old-fashioned dress, pleated and wide and to the knee. To her left stood a man and woman, whom Dirk took to be her parents, the mother holding a bundle of flowing clothes which encased a new baby. To their left and behind them stood stout relatives, presumably two aunts and three uncles. It looked like it was a christening of the new arrival. Everyone except the teenager smiled. She had a sullen look on her face, her eyes slightly averted to the right, watching something, watching something that nobody else was aware of. An involuntary groan forced itself out of Dirk's throat.

He turned the page. Another photograph of the same family, this time in a slightly different arrangement. He began turning the pages, quickening the pace; every page, both back and front, was filled up with these strangers' faces staring back at him. He felt angry, cheated, like an intruder prowling through the wrong house. Midway through the thick album, he stopped to study the faces. They suddenly seemed vaguely familiar. Something about their expressions spoke to him – there was a message here, he understood. There was an important message, a message, in fact, from his mother. It had to be. He turned the pages as quickly as was physically possible until he reached the last page. There sat a picture of himself. Himself as someone else, himself dressed head to toe in black, including old black boots, and sporting blonde hair, his skin was dark, black, but the face was still him. And he could hear a woman's voice humming the *Mockingbird* lullaby.

It was so familiar, that voice. It was, he realised, feeling sick to the pit of his stomach, his mother's voice. She was humming the lullaby right in his ears. And he was standing on a burnt

176

orange coffin, a smile on his face, the coffin taking his weight with ease, him standing on it, as if it was the most natural thing in the world. His face looked old, far older than he was, and it had a worn, lived look about it, his smile the true smile of contentment, not the usual smile of momentary happiness. It was from deep within. It spoke to him, but he could not comprehend the words. They were words of a strange language. He was straining, straining to understand, his mind racing through every foreign language word he had ever heard, screaming, willing for a familiar sound to come out of the picture's mouth, his own mouth.

Dirk woke in a cold sweat. He waved his arms about, testing, seeing if he was encased somehow. The burnt orange coffin sat before his eyes, the feet of his dream-self, clad in worn workman's boots standing on it. His mother's coffin, the one he had thrown a red rose on, had been nothing like this coffin. Her coffin was dark wood, mahogany, the man had said. Dirk had taken great care in choosing the coffin. He wanted her to go in something she would be proud to lie in. He thought of her in it now, surrounded by all the creepy crawlies she so hated.

He got up, his stretched tee-shirt hanging to above his knees as he plodded downstairs to the kitchen. He put the kettle on and while waiting for it to boil, sat down, staring at the photographs still askew on the table. He began looking through them, idly, in no particular order, and thinking back to those moments of his life. Was what the photograph portrayed really what they were feeling? Or thinking? What had prompted the taking of any one of these photographs? The notable absence of his father from them reminded him that, of course, the man practically slept with his camera. It hung, like an oversized necklace, around his neck, waiting its next use, the recording of another moment. Everything recorded for posterity. And now he, Dirk Horn, was posterity itself.

After several hours of organising the photographs into categories – one for the Horn family, one for the MacNamara family, one of him and his parents, one of his parents before he was born – tying elastic bands around them to hold them

177

together, he showered, dressed, his mind focused on each and every task as he carried it out. He put on his winter coat and, slipping his hands into his thermal gloves, walked down the quiet leafy suburban road to the familiar row of shops where nothing – and yet for him, everything – had changed.

*

It was dark and cold but Dirk continued humming *Humpty Dumpty* to himself, with an odd sense of euphoria. It was not, he knew deep inside himself, a euphoria of happiness; it was an urgent euphoria. An urgent, desperate, disparate sense of heightened awareness. It urged him on. He walked into the Long Hall, taking a deep breath. It was fairly crowded but there was a small gap at the bar into which he squeezed himself. It felt strange to be amid the buzz of chitter chatter, small talk and sociability. It felt strange and yet it felt good. The same feeling he had had in that restaurant in Rome sat with him. At ease and yet aware all was not quite right. He ordered a Guinness. It was ages since he'd had a good pint, and this was certainly the place to get one. As he wiped his freshly spilled Guinness off the grubby beer mat on the counter, he smiled at the old man huddled over his pint beside him. He wasn't sure if he was asleep or being over protective, or simply relishing every drop of the black stuff. The man grunted his acknowledgement of Dirk's presence. He took a long drink.

'You know that just before you die, now it can be an hour, it can be a day or even longer, but just before you die,' Dirk said as he elbowed the old man, 'your fingers go very white. Very white and cold. They go freezing to touch but the person will insist they have feeling in them.'

The man laughed. 'Well now, it must be near for me because me hands and me feet are cold too and would you look at the colour of them,' he said.

He let out a raucous laugh at Dirk's face. 'It's just the effect of the anaesthetic. I feel fine, honestly.'

There was something soft and gentle about his tone that made Dirk want to climb up onto his knee as he had done with his father years ago.

'What did you have done?'

'Just an old hip replaced you know. It'll happen to you, mark my words.' The man slammed his pint down on the table. 'Mark my words.' He waved at the barman. 'Same again.'

'I'm on it, Jack?' The barman nodded to Dirk. 'Alright, there?'

Dirk looked around. The two laughed.

'Will you be having another or what is bleeding wrong with you?' the barman asked.

'Ah sure, go on then, another one for the road,' said Dirk, suddenly loving the fuzzy feeling that had started to envelop him. Jack and the barman would look out for him, it was clear as day. He turned to Jack, beside him.

'So, you still feel the anaesthetic, then?'

'Oh, of course I do. Like I was still in there. The effects last up to six months? Six months, can you believe it, with that stuff racing around in your blood making you all woozy, like?'

'Six months, I didn't know that.'

'No. There's a lot of things that this old Jack knows that – what's your name?'

'Dirk.'

'Right you are. Things that this old Jack knows that Kirk doesn't know, isn't that right, Paul?' He nodded towards the barman.

'Yeah, that's right, Jack. Here you go. Two of the black stuff. On me, Jack, on me.'

'Ah now, Paul, you shouldn't be spoiling me like that.'

'Of course I will. Sure didn't we miss you when you were laid up with that blasted hip of yours. We're just glad to have you back on your feet.'

'In a manner of speaking!'

And they laughed again, Jack pointing to the crutch tucked into the leg of his stool.

Dirk realised he hadn't laughed so much since – since – and the wave of nausea hit him like a brick. He wanted to leave, to run and not stop.

'Haven't seen you around here, Kirk,' said Paul, cleaning the counter with a cloth, once white but now a pale grey. It had red stitching around the seams.

'Dirk,' said Dirk. He looked from Paul to Jack and stepped down from his stool. Why change the habit of a lifetime?

'What the fuck is that about?' said Paul, shaking his head. 'Jaysus, I've seen some queer ones in my time but that bloody bowing, now that takes the biscuit that does.'

Dirk laughed. 'It's something my mother taught me to do,' he said, smiling.

'You mother needs a good kick up the arse so she does,' said Jack, smacking his lips. 'What does she want, for you to get beaten up?'

'You okay?' Paul leaned nearer to him.

Dirk took a deep breath, his head spinning. 'Grand. Fine.'

'Is it the Guinness that's too much for you?' Jack asked, looking concerned.

'Or is it the company that's so bad?' chipped in Paul.

'No,' said Dirk, his head spinning, 'it's just I haven't been out in a while, you know, since she died.'

'Ah, lost the love of your life then. Must have been an accident. Looking at you, like, she couldn't have been more than twenty-five,' said Jack, shaking his head. 'Paul, get this boy a whiskey for his nerves, will you.'

Paul nodded, a solemn look on his face.

'Now, we'll have a toast, so we will,' said Jack, all organised. 'A toast for – what was her name?'

'Mary.' Dirk took the whiskey. It was neat, no ice, and no mixer, the pure and proper stuff in a small glass like the ones Sheila used to give him red lemonade in. He felt his head spin. He smacked his lips together, a little sup. The whiskey was good.

'Come on now, Paul, you have to have one,' said Jack.

'I'll just have a quick one now. There's a bunch of Spanish down the end there waving at me and the other fuckers behind the bar are on a fag break. They remember being kicked out for shouting at me yesterday. Nobody shouts at a barman and gets away with it!' He poured a shot into a glass for himself and raised it up.

'To Mary,' he said.

'To Mary,' Jack and Dirk chorused and downed their whiskeys in one.

They clinked their glasses and Paul went down the other end of the bar to serve the tourists.

'You know,' said Dirk, feeling a bit better, 'I was on a bus once and there was this couple arguing. They didn't even try to keep their voices down. I'm sure the whole bus was listening. And it was over something stupid. She'd spent an extra few quid on a candle so he couldn't get a pint at the pub on Saturday night. I mean how do people get like that? How do you reach the point where something so small as a couple of pennies causes an argument that is played out in public, that will be quoted in years to come. 'That time you made a show of me on the bus' I can just hear her say it.' Dirk felt upset.

Jack sighed before speaking quietly, looking directly at him. 'When you don't have much money, Dirk, even the slight wobble is like the tip that will sink the ship. I know because me and my missus frequently argued over tiny things. When you're wrapped up in things the little things are as important as the big ones.'

Dirk smiled. 'I've never had a house of my own, until now that is. I haven't had to pay bills, to try and find money for unexpected expenses – car exhausts, a broken tooth, all the little things.'

Jack was looking at him, frowning. 'Did you not live in a house with your Mary?'

Dirk nodded, thinking that Mary had been right all along; he'd no clue about living in the real world. He looked at Jack's arm resting on the bar. The hairs were standing slightly on edge; he was feeling the cold more than he admitted. He looked at the freckles on his arm. Like a child splattering paint across a kitchen floor, someone had splattered the freckles all the way up. Some were darker, more rounded, almost perfect; others were odd-shaped not round yet not anything else either, blobs of melanin blotting what could have once, long ago, been model flawless ivory skin. He shivered and he swallowed down a push of nausea.

'Jack, I've never had a missus. Mary was my mother. I had a lover once, Angela was her name. She left me after we'd climbed Croagh Patrick together. And in reality I was planning on leaving her.'

He hopped down off his stool and went to the Gents, roughly wiping the few tears away from his cheeks.

From the toilets he could hear Paul shouting 'time now, time now, time now' and he drowned the sound out with the hand-dryer. As he dried his hands he felt as if they were burning, as if the air coming out of the dryer was freezing rather than warm.

He walked back through the bar as they flashed the lights signalling last orders. He sat on the high stool beside Jack.

'I can't explain it,' Jack said, 'but there is something about them teeth of yours. I can tell a mile off. Now, while you have a foreign name and you look a bit foreign, don't ask me why, but those teeth of yours are, true as God, Catholic Irish teeth.'

Dirk shook his head. 'What do you mean I've got Catholic teeth?'

'Now, to prove it, you're going to sing with me.'

'But how can I sing if I don't know the words?'

'Aargh, of course you know the words. Everyone knows the words, sure we're born with the words etched on our minds, didn't you know that?'

'Well – '

'Why would you think you didn't know the words to *Kevin Barry*?'

'To be honest – '

'Now what other way would you be if not honest with a man like me?'

'I was brought up with a German father and he didn't like those sort of songs.'

'Your father? German? Well now. You wouldn't think to look at you. Sure you just look like me or him – '

He signalled to Paul who came over.

'What's *father* in German, then?'

'*Vati.*' Dirk smiled at Paul.

'*Vati*, he says, Jack. And here was me thinking it was *Vater*. That's what they told me when I went to Berlin a few years ago.'

'Well, it's either. It's like the difference between Daddy and Father.'

'Makes sense alright.'

'But you know, you look like anybody else around here,' continued Jack, looking around, waving his arm. 'I mean what's that got to do with anything? What about your mother, grandparents for God's sake? Did they not teach you a bit about where you came from? You know, about who you are? Do you even know who Kevin Barry was? Do they not teach you anything in school these days?'

'Of course I know who he was; he was a medical student who died on the gallows for Ireland.'

'Oh, so the German knows something then. *Sláinte*! So what did your *vati* do with you, then, if he didn't teach you rebel songs. Did he teach you German folk dancing?' He let out a roar of laughter.

Dirk smiled, shook his head. 'I never saw my father dance a day in his life,' he said. 'No, he didn't teach me anything like that. We did a tournament, once, of Scrabble.'

'Scrabble?'

'Yeah, you know the game, it's a word game, and you pick out the letters from – '

'It's for ponces,' put in Paul. 'It's a game parents make their children play so they can look intelligent.' He winked at Dirk.

'No,' said Dirk, 'I think it helped his English.'

'Being German and all that,' said Jack nodding.

'The last two?' Paul turned to Jack.

'Twist me arm, the last two.'

'These are on me,' said Dirk, 'and the two before that, too.'

'Oh, sure you're too good, too good altogether. We'll have to be seeing more of you now, after the good night we've had. Now, getting back to our Kevin. Did you know that my granddaughter Frances wrote a thesis on Kevin Barry. Yes, a thesis. She did a whole lot of research and is going to get her book published. She's in Oxford, in Oxford, England, my little Franny, right alongside all those rich people, do you hear what I'm saying? And do you know what else?'

Dirk shook his head.

'You should be looking her up instead of sitting here with the likes of me. She's another one, just like you. All alone with no one to talk to. I keep telling her to come back to the old sod. But does she listen?' He laughed and slapped Dirk on the shoulder. 'I'm off to the jacks, don't be eyeing me last pint of the night with that beady eye of yours.'

'Gotta get a move on, time's up now.'

Dirk followed the grubby grey cloth as Paul swept it back and forth across the counter. He looked around. Even the Spanish crowd had left.

'Now Jack, we have this conversation nearly every night,' Paul said as Jack hauled himself up on his seat, his chequered jacket looking not unlike the pattern on the material of the stool.

'Are you trying to tell me something? Trying to shame me in front of my new German friend?'

Paul laughed. 'I'll start again, now. Now. We have this conversation every evening.'

'Not every evening, only when I'm here. I'm hardly here every evening, now, come on, would you!'

'True, true enough for you, right. I'll just ask you again. Do you have no bleeding home to go to?'

Jack nearly fell off his stool laughing.

'Would you listen to him. Jaysus. Bellowing at me like that, like I was half way down the room! No bleeding home to go to. I mean, really and truly.'

'How are you getting home?' Dirk could feel a panic rising inside him.

'Jack'll get home the way he always gets home.' Paul squeezed out the cloth into a sink that Dirk hadn't noticed until now. 'With a shove and a push!'

Jack smacked his lips. 'That's me done and dusted. What about you?'

'Nearly.' Dirk drank the rest of his pint quickly.

'Thank fuck,' said Paul. 'Now I can get some bleeding shut eye.'

'If that's all the thanks we get for our custom we won't be

coming here again,' said Jack.

'Ah get outta here, will you? Go on, skedaddle!'

'Give me a hand, Dirk, now would you?'

'Of course!'

Dirk helped Jack with his one crutch and, with the free arm, Jack linked Dirk's arm.

'Bye now and thanks a million for everything,' Dirk shouted back to Paul.

'Yeah, yeah, yeah,' said Paul as he followed them to the door, shutting it with a sharp click as they stepped outside.

They were on an almost deserted South Great George's Street. A few were wandering home, arms outstretched towards the road in the hope that an empty taxi would pass by and pick them up.

'You know, Jack,' Dirk said, stopping and turning to face him, 'I've reached my point of no return and I'm making myself return. Do you understand what I'm saying? I am forcing myself to return.'

'To return to where? What are you talking about, for God's sake?'

'To return to myself.' Dirk released Jack and began twirling, arms outstretched, shouting as he did so. 'To return to the little boy lost in a childhood photo. It was taken on St Patrick's Day, on my dad's shoulders, proud as punch I was. And I always like to tell myself that he was proud as well. Proud to have me as his son.'

'But you still can't sing a song, boy, can you?'

Dirk stopped twirling. 'You start, then, go on.'

Jack cleared his throat. 'Now normally I'd have a few whiskeys to lubricate the auld vocal cords now, but sure it's only you and me now so here we go.

In Mountjoy Jail one Monday morning
High upon the gallows tree — '

'Jesus, Jack, you can't reach those high notes at all.'

'I know, I know, sure let me try again. Give me a chance now.' Jack cleared his throat again.

'*...high upon the gallows tree*
Kevin Barry gave his young life

185

For the cause of liberty.
Just a lad of eighteen summers
You see, he was eighteen, Dirk, not nineteen,' Jack said.

'Wait,' said Dirk, 'you know it wasn't on my dad's shoulders. I took the photo out the other day and it was on mother's shoulders that I sat. Big lump that I was. Why wasn't I on my father's shoulders like other children, I ask?'

'Is me singing not good enough for you to give me the courtesy to listen to it?'

'No, no it's not that, just thinking about Kevin Barry and the photograph, him holding his head up high – '

'Because he knew what he stood for, he knew what he was fighting for.'

'Yeah. Yeah.'

'What are you fighting for? What do you want?'

Dirk shrugged his shoulders. 'I don't know. I mean, look at all these silent people,' Dirk continued, linking Jack and walking towards Camden Street. 'Do you think any one of them would stop and talk? Stop and ask if you were okay? If you were happy? Or if you had just lost somebody? I lost a twin, a sister my mother never even saw. Lost! Now *that's* a funny one. As if I just lost my mother. Just like that. Where's she gone? Six feet under, oops, I've just lost my mother.'

'I'm up here. At the flats by the bridge.'

'Sure,' said Dirk. 'I might even carry on and find myself somewhere else to go along the way home. Maybe get myself a bag of chips.'

'If only my Franny'd come home from Oxford.'

'She will, you know,' Dirk said, sure of it. 'But only when the time is right for her. Everything has its own rhythm. Goes at its own time.'

'Right you are, Dirk. Right you are. You know for such a fella wrapped in cotton wool, there's something about you that I can't put me finger on. Something niggling, not quite right, if you don't mind me being honest with you.'

'Maybe,' said Dirk, slowly. 'Maybe, that's just who I am.'

Happiness Comes From Nowhere

The sliding happens so fast you don't know you've reached the end. At first it's like a box around you, like a bad headache you can't shake. So you take a drink and feel a measure of release. Then you feel that inexplicable numbness creep over you and you shout at yourself – *Quick! Rid yourself! Of yourself! Feel something! Anything!* – And you do. You take another drink. Or a puff or whatever is handy for you. Ah.

The amazing thing is that it works. The sliding stops – like when you were a kid and the rubber soles on your shoes stopped you from sliding down the slide – and you're on a par with everyone else. And you smile and chat and kiss and fuck and work and shit. Happiness. It's a smooth ride.

And then one day, none of these things work.

You wander, a ghost.

You drink cheap wine, try alcohol far more expensive than you can afford, knock back pints, bitter on your tongue, jive dance, have quickies in bed, try lingering mornings slowly making love. But still. Still. Your heart is numb.

You have become transparent.

You see nothing but fear in everything.

And you have to look at your reflection in the sober light of day.

And realise that there is no going back.

There is only going forward.

The cardboard box that your new television was packed in sits compactly in the centre of the living room. It wills you to climb inside, this faux womb of modern entertainment. You rub your eyes, staring at it, the palpitations beating against your ribcage, your consciousness screaming. It screams at you to open that black box – the one you always knew was there. The one that everyone has, the one with the rusty clasp that was hastily shut at some stage when they were a kid, the one that is stuffed full of memories, that every now and then scratch at the lid during a drunken moment, that scream to be let out.

The cardboard is somewhat battered, like an old man's face, the lines telling the recent and forgotten history. Everyone has someone they can cry with. A God incarnate, listening post, Wailing Wall, light; the boy you were for your father, the girl you wanted to be for your mother.

When the shadows at the recesses of your mind leap forward, enthusiastically bound to shoot you down, you consciously push them back, telling yourself again and again that no, your story was a story that had to be told.

Happiness comes from nowhere.

You surprise even yourself when you awake and realise that you have actually slept in the cardboard box in the living room, not a curtain in sight drawn. All laid bare for the neighbours to have a good ogle. You slowly stretch out, foot by foot breaking through the cardboard, and remember – with what seems like a momentary stop of your heart – what you'd done the day before. You have…

…let go.

Acknowledgements

Some (or versions) of these chapters first appeared in *Census 3: The Third Seven Towers Anthology*, *TheFirstCut* (Issues 3 and 5), *Cobalt Review* (Spring 2012).

Thanks go to my writing friends Sarah Broughton and Karen Lee Street for endless hours of reading and debating the psyche of the characters in this novel. Thanks also to those I met during my time at the University of Glamorgan, and to others who have commented on my work, especially Anne Boland, Bríd Connolly, Tony Cunningham, Catherine Merriman, Mary Ryan, Phil Saul, Hazel Stanley. Particularly large thanks to Noel Duffy for brave suggestions, keen insights and for just getting it.

Some of this novel was written at the colourful desks of Fighting Words in Dublin: my gratitude goes to those who run this centre and to all who write there.

Parts were also fine-tuned in residency at The Tyrone Guthrie Centre at Annaghmakerrig. To all who make it such a wonderful place I would like to express my appreciation.

A special thanks to Sheila Barrett whose encouragement I still carry with me; and to Philip Gross and Sheenagh Pugh for their support from near and far.

Heartfelt gratitude to Rob Middlehurst for his *writerly reader's eye* and for pushing the instinctual. For his guidance, I will be forever indebted.

A deep thank you to Adele Ward and Mike Fortune-Wood at Ward Wood Publishing for taking my writing on; for their courage, editorial guidance and a great design flair.

About the Author

Born in Dublin, Ireland, Shauna has worked and lived in Mexico, Spain, India and the UK. She currently lives in County Kildare. Her fiction has been published widely and she has given public readings and presented on writing in Ireland, the UK, Germany and the USA. *Happiness Comes From Nowhere* is her first novel.